Letters to Dead Authors

Andrew Lang

Letters to Dead Authors

Copyright © 2020 Bibliotech Press
All rights reserved

ISBN: 978-1-64799-621-5

Contents

Preface

Sixteen of these Letters, which were written at the suggestion of the editor of the 'St. James's Gazette,' appeared in that journal, from which they are now reprinted, by the editor's kind permission. They have been somewhat emended, and a few additions have been made. The Letters to Horace, Byron, Isaak Walton, Chapelain, Ronsard, and Theocritus have not been published before.

The gem published for the first time on the title-page is a red cornelian in the British Museum, probably Graeco-Roman, and treated in an archaistic style. It represents Hermes Psychogogos, with a Soul, and has some likeness to the Baptism of Our Lord, as usually shown in art. Perhaps it may be post-Christian. The gem was selected by Mr. A. S. Murray.

It is, perhaps, superfluous to add that some of the Letters are written rather to suit the Correspondent than to express the writer's own taste or opinions. The Epistle to Lord Byron, especially, is 'writ in a manner which is my aversion.'

I

To W. M. Thackeray

Sir,—There are many things that stand in the way of the critic when he has a mind to praise the living. He may dread the charge of writing rather to vex a rival than to exalt the subject of his applause. He shuns the appearance of seeking the favour of the famous, and would not willingly be regarded as one of the many parasites who now advertise each movement and action of contemporary genius. 'Such and such men of letters are passing their summer holidays in the Val d'Aosta,' or the Mountains of the Moon, or the Suliman Range, as it may happen. So reports our literary 'Court Circular,' and all our Précieuses read the tidings with enthusiasm. Lastly, if the critic be quite new to the world of letters, he may superfluously fear to vex a poet or a novelist by the abundance of his eulogy. No such doubts perplex us when, with all our hearts, we would commend the departed; for they have passed almost beyond the reach even of envy; and to those pale cheeks of theirs no commendation can bring the red.

You, above all others, were and remain without a rival in your many-sided excellence, and praise of you strikes at none of those who have survived your day. The increase of time only mellows your renown, and each year that passes and brings you no successor does but sharpen the keenness of our sense of loss. In what other novelist, since Scott was worn down by the burden of a forlorn endeavour, and died for honour's sake, has the world found

1

so many of the fairest gifts combined? If we may not call you a poet (for the first of English writers of light verse did not seek that crown), who that was less than a poet ever saw life with a glance so keen as yours, so steady, and so sane? Your pathos was never cheap, your laughter never forced; your sigh was never the pulpit trick of the preacher. Your funny people—your Costigans and Fokers—were not mere characters of trick and catch-word, were not empty comic masks. Behind each the human heart was beating; and ever and again we were allowed to see the features of the man.

Thus fiction in your hands was not simply a profession, like another, but a constant reflection of the whole surface of life: a repeated echo of its laughter and its complaint. Others have written, and not written badly, with the stolid professional regularity of the clerk at his desk; you, like the Scholar Gipsy, might have said that 'it needs heaven-sent moments for this skill.' There are, it will not surprise you, some honourable women and a few men who call you a cynic; who speak of 'the withered world of Thackerayan satire;' who think your eyes were ever turned to the sordid aspects of life—to the mother-in-law who threatens to 'take away her silver bread-basket;' to the intriguer, the sneak, the termagant; to the Beckys, and Barnes Newcomes, and Mrs. Mackenzies of this world. The quarrel of these sentimentalists is really with life, not with you; they might as wisely blame Monsieur Buffon because there are snakes in his Natural History. Had you not impaled certain noxious human insects, you would have better pleased Mr. Ruskin; had you confined yourself to such performances, you would have been more dear to the Neo-Balzacian school in fiction.

You are accused of never having drawn a good woman who was not a doll, but the ladies that bring this charge seldom remind us

2

either of Lady Castlewood or of Theo or Hetty Lambert. The best women can pardon you Becky Sharp and Blanche Amory; they find it harder to forgive you Emmy Sedley and Helen Pendennis. Yet what man does not know in his heart that the best women—God bless them—lean, in their characters, either to the sweet passiveness of Emmy or to the sensitive and jealous affections of Helen? 'Tis Heaven, not you, that made them so; and they are easily pardoned, both for being a very little lower than the angels and for their gentle ambition to be painted, as by Guido or Guercino, with wings and harps and haloes. So ladies have occasionally seen their own faces in the glass of fancy, and, thus inspired, have drawn Romola and Consuelo. Yet when these fair idealists, Mdme. Sand and George Eliot, designed Rosamund Vincy and Horace, was there not a spice of malice in the portraits which we miss in your least favourable studies?

That the creator of Colonel Newcome and of Henry Esmond was a snarling cynic; that he who designed Rachel Esmond could not draw a good woman: these are the chief charges (all indifferent now to you, who were once so sensitive) that your admirers have to contend against. A French critic, M. Taine, also protests that you do preach too much. Did any author but yourself so frequently break the thread (seldom a strong thread) of his plot to converse with his reader and moralise his tale, we also might be offended. But who that loves Montaigne and Pascal, who that likes the wise trifling of the one and can bear with the melancholy of the other, but prefers your preaching to another's playing!

Your thoughts come in, like the intervention of the Greek Chorus, as an ornament and source of fresh delight. Like the songs of the Chorus, they bid us pause a moment over the wider laws and actions of human fate and human life, and we turn from your

3

persons to yourself, and again from yourself to your persons, as from the odes of Sophocles or Aristophanes to the action of their characters on the stage. Nor, to my taste, does the mere music and melancholy dignity of your style in these passages of meditation fall far below the highest efforts of poetry. I remember that scene where Clive, at Barnes Newcome's Lecture on the Poetry of the Affections, sees Ethel who is lost to him. 'And the past and its dear histories, and youth and its hopes and passions, and tones and looks for ever echoing in the heart and present in the memory — these, no doubt, poor Clive saw and heard as he looked across the great gulf of time, and parting and grief, and beheld the wonmn he had loved for many years.'

For ever echoing in the heart and present in the memory: who has not heard these tones, who does not hear them as he turns over your books that, for so many years, have been his companions and comforters? We have been young and old, we have been sad and merry with you, we have listened to the mid-night chimes with Pen and Warrington, have stood with you beside the death-bed, have mourned at that yet more awful funeral of lost love, and with you have prayed in the inmost chapel sacred to our old and immortal affections, a' léal souvenir! And whenever you speak for yourself, and speak in earnest, how magical, how rare, how lonely in our literature is the beauty of your sentences! 'I can't express the charm of them' (so you write of George Sand; so we may write of you): 'they seem to me like the sound of country bells, provoking I don't know what vein of music and meditation, and falling sweetly and sadly on the ear.' Surely that style, so fresh, so rich, so full of surprises — that style which stamps as classical your fragments of slang, and perpetually astonishes and delights — would alone give immortality to an author, even had he little to say. But you, with

4

your whole wide world of fops and fools, of good women and brave men, of honest absurdities and cheery adventurers: you who created the Steynes and Newcomes, the Beckys and Blanches, Captain Costigan and F. B., and the Chevalier Strong—all that host of friends imperishable—you must survive with Shakespeare and Cervantes in the memory and affection of men.

II

To Charles Dickens

Sir,—It has been said that every man is born a Platonist or an Aristotelian, though the enormous majority of us, to be sure, live and die without being conscious of any invidious philosophic partiality whatever. With more truth (though that does not imply very much) every Englishman who reads may be said to be a partisan of yourself or of Mr. Thackeray. Why should there be any partisanship in the matter; and why, having two such good things as your novels and those of your contemporary, should we not be silently happy in the possession? Well, men are made so, and must needs fight and argue over their tastes in enjoyment. For myself, I may say that in this matter I am what the Americans do not call a 'Mugwump,' what English politicians dub a 'superior person'—that is, I take no side, and attempt to enjoy the best of both.

It must be owned that this attitude is sometimes made a little difficult by the vigour of your special devotees. They have ceased, indeed, thank Heaven! to imitate you; and even in 'descriptive articles' the touch of Mr. Gigadibs, of him whom 'we almost took for the true Dickens,' has disappeared. The young lions of the Press no longer mimic your less admirable mannerisms—do not strain so much after fantastic comparisons, do not (in your manner and Mr. Carlyle's) give people nick-names derived from their teeth, or their complexion; and, generally, we are spared second-hand copies of all that in your style was least to be commended. But, though

6

improved by lapse of time in this respect, your devotees still put on little conscious airs of virtue, robust manliness, and so forth, which would have irritated you very much, and there survive some press men who seem to have read you a little (especially your later works), and never to have read anything else. Now familiarity with the pages of 'Our Mutual Friend'and 'Dombey and Son' does not precisely constitute a liberal education, and the assumption that it does is apt (quite unreasonably) to prejudice people against the greatest comic genius of modern times.

On the other hand, Time is at last beginning to sift the true admirers of Dickens from the false. Yours, Sir, in the best sense of the word, is a popular success, a popular reputation. For example, I know that, in a remote and even Pictish part of this kingdom, a rural household, humble and under the shadow of a sorrow inevitably approaching, has found in 'David Copperfield' oblivion of winter, of sorrow, and of sickness. On the other hand, people are now picking up heart to say that 'they cannot read Dickens,' and that they particularly detest 'Pickwick.' I believe it was young ladies who first had the courage of their convictions in this respect. 'Tout sied aux belles,' and the fair, in the confidence of youth, often venture on remarkable confessions. In your 'Natural History of Young Ladies' I do not remember that you describe the Humorous Young Lady[1]. She is a very rare bird indeed, and humour generally is at a deplorably low level in England.

Hence come all sorts of mischief, arisen since you left us; and, it may be said, that inordinate philanthropy, genteel sympathy with Irish murder and arson, Societies for Badgering the Poor, Esoteric

---

[1] I am informed that the Natural History of Young Ladies is attributed, by some writers, to another philosopher, the author of The Art of Pluck.

Buddhism, and a score of other plagues, including what was once called Aestheticism, are all, primarily, due to want of humour. People discuss, with the gravest faces, matters which properly should only be stated as the wildest paradoxes. It naturally follows that, in a period almost destitute of humour, many respectable persons 'cannot read Dickens,' and are not ashamed to glory in their shame. We ought not to be angry with others for their misfortunes; and yet when one meets the crétins who boast that they cannot read Dickens, one certainly does feel much as Mr. Samuel Weller felt when he encountered Mr. Job Trotter.

How very singular has been the history of the decline of humour. Is there any profound psychological truth to be gathered from consideration of the fact that humour has gone out with cruelty? A hundred years ago, eighty years ago—nay, fifty years ago—we were a cruel but also a humorous people. We had bull-baitings, and badger-drawings, and hustings, and prize-fights, and cock-fights; we went to see men hanged; the pillory and the stocks were no empty 'terrors unto evil-doers,' for there was commonly a malefactor occupying each of these institutions. With all this we had a broad blown comic sense. We had Ho-garth, and Bunbury, and George Cruikshank, and Gilray; we had Leech and Surtees, and the creator of Tittlebat Titmouse; we had the Shepherd of the 'Noctes,' and, above all, we had you.

From the old giants of English fun—burly persons delighting in broad caricature, in decided colours, in cockney jokes, in swashing blows at the more prominent and obvious human follies—from these you derived the splendid high spirits and unhesitating mirth of your earlier works. Mr. Squeers, and Sam Weller, and Mrs. Gamp, and all the Pickwickians, and Mr. Dowler, and John Browdie—these and their immortal companions were reared, so to

8

speak, on the beef and beer of that naughty, fox-hunting, badger-baiting old England, which we have improved out of existence. And these characters, assuredly, are your best; by them, though stupid people cannot read about them, you will live while there is a laugh left among us. Perhaps that does not assure you a very prolonged existence, but only the future can show.

The dismal seriousness of the time cannot, let us hope, last for ever and a day. Honest old Laughter, the true lutin of your inspiration, must have life left in him yet, and cannot die; though it is true that the taste for your pathos, and your melodrama, and plots constructed after your favourite fashion ('Great Expectations' and the 'Tale of Two Cities' are exceptions) may go by and never be regretted. Were people simpler, or only less clear-sighted, as far as your pathos is concerned, a generation ago? Jeffrey, the hard-headed shallow critic, who declared that Wordsworth 'would never do,' cried, 'wept like anything,' over your Little Nell. One still laughs as heartily as ever with Dick Swiveller; but who can cry over Little Nell?

Ah, Sir, how could you—who knew so intimately, who remembered so strangely well the fancies, the dreams, the sufferings of childhood—how could you 'wallow naked in the pathetic,' and massacre holocausts of the Innocents? To draw tears by gloating over a child's death-bed, was it worthy of you? Was it the kind of work over which our hearts should melt? I confess that Little Nell might die a dozen times, and be welcomed by whole legions of Angels, and I (like the bereaved fowl mentioned by Pet Marjory) would remain unmoved.

> *She was more than usual calm,*
> *She did not give a single dam,*

9

wrote the astonishing child who diverted the leisure of Scott. Over your Little Nell and your Little Dombey I remain more than usual calm; and probably so do thousands of your most sincere admirers. But about matter of this kind, and the unsealing of the fountains of tears, who can argue? Where is taste? where is truth? What tears are 'manly, Sir, manly,' as Fred Bayham has it; and of what lamentations ought we rather to be ashamed? Sunt lacrymae rerum; one has been moved in the cell where Socrates tasted the hemlock; or by the river-banks where Syracusan arrows slew the parched Athenians among the mire and blood; or, in fiction, when Colonel Newcome said Adsum, or over the diary of Clare Doria Forey, or where Aramis laments, with strange tears, the death of Porthos. But over Dombey (the Son), or Little Nell, one declines to snivel.

When an author deliberately sits down and says, 'Now, let us have a good cry,' he poisons the wells of sensibility and chokes, at least in many breasts, the fountain of tears. Out of 'Dombey and Son' there is little we care to remember except the deathless Mr. Toots; just as we forget the melodramatics of 'Martin Chuzzlewit.' I have read in that book a score of times; I never see it but I revel in it—in Pecksniff, and Mrs. Gamp, and the Americans. But what the plot is all about, what Jonas did, what Montagu Tigg had to make in the matter, what all the pictures with plenty of shading illustrate, I have never been able to comprehend. In the same way, one of your most thorough-going admirers has allowed (in the licence of private conversation) that 'Ralph Nickleby and Monk are too steep;' and probably a cultivated taste will always find them a little precipitous.

'Too steep:'—the slang expresses that defect of an ardent genius, carried above itself, and out of the air we breathe, both in its grotesque and in its gloomy imaginations. To force the note, to

10

press fantasy too hard, to deepen the gloom with black over the indigo, that was the failing which proved you mortal. To take an instance in little: when Pip went to Mr. Pumblechook's, the boy thought the seedsman 'a very happy man to have so many little drawers in his shop.' The reflection is thoroughly boyish; but then you add, 'I wondered whether the flower-seeds and bulbs ever wanted of a fine day to break out of those jails and bloom.' That is not boyish at all; that is the hard-driven, jaded literary fancy at work.

'So we arraign her; but she,' the Genius of Charles Dickens, how brilliant, how kindly, how beneficent she is! dwelling by a fountain of laughter imperishable; though there is something of an alien salt in the neighbouring fountain of tears. How poor the world of fancy would be, how 'dispeopled of her dreams,' if, in some ruin of the social system, the books of Dickens were lost; and if The Dodger, and Charley Bates, and Mr. Crinkle, and Miss Squeers, and Sam Weller, and Mrs. Gamp, and Dick Swiveller were to perish, or to vanish with Menander's men and women! We cannot think of our world without them; and, children of dreams as they are, they seem more essential than great statesmen, artists, soldiers, who have actually worn flesh and blood, ribbons and orders, gowns and uniforms. May we not almost welcome 'Free Education'? for every Englishman who can read, unless he be an Ass, is a reader the more for you.

III

To Pierre de Ronsard (Prince of Poets)

Master and Prince of Poets, — As we know what choice thou madest of a sepulchre (a choice how ill fulfilled by the jealousy of Fate), so we know well the manner of thy chosen immortality. In the Plains Elysian, among the heroes and the ladies of old song, there was thy Love with thee to enjoy her paradise in an eternal spring.

> *La' du plaisant Avril la saison imortelle*
> *Sans eschange le suit,*
> *La terre sans labeur, de sa grasse mamelle,*
> *Tout chose y produit;*
> *D'enbas la troupe sainte autrefois amoureuse,*
> *Nous honorant sur tous,*
> *Viendra nous saluer, s'estimant bien-heureuse*
> *De s'accointer de nous.*

There thou dwellest, with the learned lovers of old days, with Belleau, and Du Bellay, and Bai'f, and the flower of the maidens of Anjou. Surely no rumour reaches thee, in that happy place of reconciled affections, no rumour of the rudeness of Time, the despite of men, and the change which stole from thy locks, so early grey, the crown of laurels and of thine own roses. How different from thy choice of a sepulchre have been the fortunes of thy tomb!

> *I will that none should break*
> *The marble for my sake,*

> Wishful to make more fair
>> My sepulchre.

So didst thou sing, or so thy sweet numbers run in my rude English. Wearied
of Courts and of priories, thou didst desire a grave beside thine own
Loire, not remote from

> The caves, the founts that fall
> From the high mountain wall,
> That fall and flash and fleet,
>> Wilh silver fret.

> Only a laurel tree
> Shall guard the grave of me;
> Only Apollo's bough
> Shall shade me now!

Far other has been thy sepulchre: not in the free air, among the field
flowers, but in thy priory of Saint Cosme, with marble for a monument,
and no green grass to cover thee. Restless wert thou in thy life; thy
dust was not to be restful in thy death. The Huguenots, ces nouveaux
Chrétiens qui la France ont pillée, destroyed thy tomb, and the warning
of the later monument,

ABI, NEFASTE, QUAM CALCAS HUMUM SACRA EST,

has not scared away malicious men. The storm that passed over
France a hundred years ago, more terrible than the religious wars
that thou didst weep for, has swept the column from the tomb. The
marble was broken by violent hands, and the shattered sepulchre of
the Prince of Poets gained a dusty hospitality from the museum of a

13

country town. Better had been the laurel of thy desire, the creeping vine, and the ivy tree.

Scarce more fortunate, for long, than thy monument was thy memory. Thou hast not encountered, Master, in the Paradise of Poets, Messieurs Malherbe, De Balzac, and Boileau—Boileau who spoke of thee as Ce poéte orgueilleux trébuché de si haut!

These gallant gentlemen, I make no doubt, are happy after their own fashion, backbiting each other and thee in the Paradise of Critics. In their time they wrought thee much evil, grumbling that thou wrotest in Greek and Latin (of which tongues certain of them had but little skill), and blaming thy many lyric melodies and the free flow of thy lines. What said M. de Balzac to M. Chapelain? 'M. de Malherbe, M. de Grasse, and yourself must be very little poets, if Ronsard be a great one.' Time has brought in his revenges, and Messieurs Chapelain and De Grasse are as well forgotten as thou art well remembered. Men could not always be deaf to thy sweet old songs, nor blind to the beauty of thy roses and thy loves. When they took the wax out of their ears that M. Boileau had given them lest they should hear the singing of thy Sirens, then they were deaf no longer, then they heard the old deaf poet singing and made answer to his lays. Hast thou not heard these sounds? have they not reached thee, the voices and the lyres of Théophile Gautier and Alfred de Musset? Methinks thou hast marked them, and been glad that the old notes were ringing again and the old French lyric measures tripping to thine ancient harmonies, echoing and replying to the Muses of Horace and Catullus. Returning to Nature, poets returned to thee. Thy monument has perished, but not thy music, and the Prince of Poets has returned to his own again in a glorious Restoration.

Through the dust and smoke of ages, and through the centuries of wars we strain our eyes and try to gain a glimpse of thee, Master, in thy good days, when the Muses walked with thee. We seem to mark thee wandering silent through some little village, or dreaming in the woods, or loitering among thy lonely places, or in gardens where the roses blossom among wilder flowers, or on river banks where the whispering poplars and sighing reeds make answer to the murmur of the waters. Such a picture hast thou drawn of thyself in the summer afternoons.

> *Je m'en vais pourmener tantost parmy la plaine,*
> *Tantost en un village, et tantost en un bois,*
> *Et tantost par les lieux solitaires et cois.*
> *J'aime fort les jardins qui sentent le sauvage,*
> *J'aime le flot de l'eau qui gazou'ille au rivage.*

Still, methinks, there was a book in the hand of the grave and learned poet; still thou wouldst carry thy Horace, thy Catullus, thy Theocritus, through the gem-like weather of the Renouveau, when the woods were enamelled with flowers, and the young Spring was lodged, like a wandering prince, in his great palaces hung with green:

> *Orgueilleux de ses fleurs, enflé de sa jeunesse,*
> *Logé comme un grand Prince en ses vertes maisons!*

Thou sawest, in these woods by Loire side, the fair shapes of old religion, Fauns, Nymphs, and Satyrs, and heard'st in the nightingale's music the plaint of Philomel. The ancient poets came back in the train of thyself and of the Spring, and learning was scarce less dear to thee than love; and thy ladies seemed fairer for the names they borrowed from the beauties of forgotten days, Helen and Cassandra. How sweetly didst thou sing to them thine old morality, and how gravely didst thou teach the lesson of the

Roses! Well didst thou know it, well didst thou love the Rose, since thy nurse, carrying thee, an infant, to the holy font, let fall on thee the sacred water brimmed with floating blossoms of the Rose!

> *Mignonne, allons voir si la Rose,*
> *Qui ce matin avoit desclose*
> *Sa robe de pourpre au soleil,*
> *A point perdu ceste vespree*
> *Les plis de sa robe pourpree,*
> *Et son teint au votre pareil.*

And again,

> *La belle Rose du Printemps,*
> *Aubert, admoneste les hommes*
> *Passer joyeusement le temps,*
> *Et pendant que jeunes nous sommes,*
> *Esbattre la fleur de nos ans.*

In the same mood, looking far down the future, thou sangest of thy lady's age, the most sad, the most beautiful of thy sad and beautiful lays; for if thy bees gathered much honey 't was somewhat bitter to taste, as that of the Sardinian yews. How clearly we see the great hall, the grey lady spinning and humming among her drowsy maids, and how they waken at the word, and she sees her spring in their eyes, and they forecast their winter in her face, when she murmurs "Twas Ronsard sang of me.'

Winter, and summer, and spring, how swiftly they pass, and how early time brought thee his sorrows, and grief cast her dust upon thy head.

> *Adieu ma Lyre, adieu fillettes,*
> *Jadis mes douces amourettes,*

Adieu, je sens venir ma fin,
Nul passetemps de ma jeunesse
Ne m'accompagne en la vieillesse,
Que le feu, le lict et le vin.

Wine, and a soft bed, and a bright fire: to this trinity of poor pleasures we come soon, if, indeed, wine be left to us. Poetry herself deserts us; is it not said that Bacchus never forgives a renegade? and most of us turn recreants to Bacchus. Even the bright fire, I fear, was not always there to warm thine old blood, Master, or, if fire there were, the wood was not bought with thy book-seller's money. When autumn was drawing in during thine early old age, in 1584, didst thou not write that thou hadst never received a sou at the hands of all the publishers who vended thy books? And as thou wert about putting forth the folio edition of 1584, thou didst pray Buon, the bookseller, to give thee sixty crowns to buy wood withal, and make thee a bright fire in winter weather, and comfort thine old age with thy friend Gallandius. And if Buon will not pay, then to try the other book-sellers, 'that wish to take everything and give nothing.'

Was it knowledge of this passage, Master, or ignorance of everything else, that made certain of the common steadfast dunces of our days speak of thee as if thou hadst been a starveling, neglected poetaster, jealous forsooth, of Maitre Francoys Rabelais? See how ignorantly M. Fleury writes, who teaches French literature withal to them of Muscovy, and hath indited a Life of Rabelais. 'Rabelais était revétu d'un emploi honorable; Ronsard était traité en subalterne,' quoth this wondrous professor. What! Pierre de Ronsard, a gentleman of a noble house, holding the revenue of many abbeys, the friend of Mary Stuart, of the Duc d'Orléans, of Charles IX., he is traité en subalterne, and is jealous of a frocked or

17

unfrocked manant like Maitre Francoys! And then this amazing Fleury falls foul of thine epitaph on Mai'tre Francoys and cries, 'Ronsard a voulu faire des vers méchants; il n'a fait que de méchants vers.' More truly saith M. Sainte-Beuve, 'If the good Rabelais had returned to Meudon on the day when this epitaph was made over the wine, he would, methinks, have laughed heartily.' But what shall be said of a Professor like the egregious M. Fleury, who holds that Ronsard was despised at Court? Was there a party at tennis when the king would not fain have had thee on his side, declaring that he ever won when Ronsard was his partner? Did he not give thee benefices, and many priories, and call thee his father in Apollo, and even, so they say, bid thee sit down beside him on his throne? Away, ye scandalous folk, who tell us that there was strife between the Prince of Poets and the King of Mirth. Naught have ye by way of proof of your slander but the talk of Jean Bernier, a scurrilous, starveling apothecary, who put forth his fables in 1697, a century and a half after Mai'tre Francoys died. Bayle quoted this fellow in a note, and ye all steal the tattle one from another in your dull manner, and know not whence it comes, nor even that Bayle would none of it and mocked its author. With so little knowledge is history written, and thus doth each chattering brook of a 'Life swell with its tribute, that great Mississippi of falsehood,' Biography.

IV

To Herodotus

To Herodotus of Halicarnassus, greeting.—Concerning the matters set forth in your histories, and the tales you tell about both Greeks and barbarians, whether they be true, or whether they be false, men dispute not little but a great deal. Wherefore I, being concerned to know the verity, did set forth to make search in every manner, and came in my quest even unto the ends of the earth. For there is an island of the Cimmerians beyond the Straits of Heracles, some three days' voyage to a ship that hath a fair following wind in her sails; and there it is said that men know many things from of old: thither, then, I came in my inquiry. Now, the island is not small, but large, greater than the whole of Hellas; and they call it Britain. In that island the east wind blows for ten parts of the year, and the people know not how to cover themselves from the cold. But for the other two months of the year the sun shines fiercely, so that some of them die thereof, and others die of the frozen mixed drinks; for they have ice even in the summer, and this ice they put to their liquor. Through the whole of this island, from the west even to the east, there flows a river called Thames: a great river and a laborious, but not to be likened to the River of Egypt.

The mouth of this river, where I stepped out from my ship, is exceedingly foul and of an evil savour by reason of the city on the banks. Now this city is several hundred parasangs in circumference. Yet a man that needed not to breathe the air might

19

go round it in one hour, in chariots that run under the earth; and these chariots are drawn by creatures that breathe smoke and sulphur, such as Orpheus mentions in his 'Argonautica,' if it be by Orpheus. The people of the town, when I inquired of them concerning Herodotus of Halicarnassus, looked on me with amazement, and went straightway about their business,—namely, to seek out whatsoever new thing is coming to pass all over the whole inhabited world, and as for things old, they take no keep of them.

Nevertheless, by diligence I learned that he who in this land knew most concerning Herodotus was a priest, and dwelt in the priests' city on the river which is called the City of the Ford of the Ox. But whether Io, when she wore a cow's shape, had passed by that way in her wanderings, and thence comes the name of that city, I could not (though I asked all men I met) learn aught with certainty. But to me, considering this, it seemed that Io must have come thither. And now farewell to Io.

To the City of the Priests there are two roads: one by land; and one by water, following the river. To a well-girdled man, the land journey is but one day's travel; by the river it is longer but more pleasant. Now that river flows, as I said, from the west to the east. And there is in it a fish called chub, which they catch; but they do not eat it, for a certain sacred reason. Also there is a fish called trout, and this is the manner of his catching. They build far this purpose great dams of wood, which they call weirs. Having built the weir they sit upon it with rods in their hands, and a line on the rod, and at the end of the line a little fish. There then they 'sit and spin in the sun,' as one of their poets says, not for a short time but for many days, having rods in their hands and eating and drinking. In this wise they angle for the fish called trout; but whether they

20

ever catch him or not, not having seen it, I cannot say; for it is not pleasant to me to speak things concerning which I know not the truth.

Now, after sailing and rowing against the stream for certain days, I came to the City of the Ford of the Ox. Here the river changes his name, and is called Isis, after the name of the goddess of the Egyptians. But whether the Britons brought the name from Egypt or whether the Egyptians took it from the Britons, not knowing I prefer not to say. But to me it seems that the Britons are a colony of the Egyptians, or the Egyptians a colony of the Britons. Moreover, when I was in Egypt I saw certain soldiers in white helmets, who were certainly British. But what they did there (as Egypt neither belongs to Britain nor Britain to Egypt) I know not, neither could they tell me. But one of them replied to me in that line of Homer (if the Odyssey be Homer's), 'We have come to a sorry Cyprus, and a sad Egypt.' Others told me that they once marched against the Ethiopians, and having defeated them several times, then came back again, leaving their property to the Ethiopians. But as to the truth of this I leave it to every man to form his own opinion.

Having come into the City of the Priests, I went forth into the street, and found a priest of the baser sort, who for a piece of silver led me hither and thither among the temples, discoursing of many things.

Now it seemed to me a strange thing that the city was empty, and no man dwelling therein, save a few priests only, and their wives, and their children, who are drawn to and fro in little carriages dragged by women, but the priest told me that during half the year the city was desolate, for that there came somewhat called 'The Long,' or 'The Vac,' and drave out the young priests. And he said that these did no other thing but row boats, and throw balls from

21

one to the other, and this they were made to do, he said, that the young priests might learn to be humble, for they are the proudest of men. But whether he spoke truth or not I know not, only I set down what he told me. But to anyone considering it, this appears rather to jump with his story—namely, that the young priests have houses on the river, painted of divers colours, all of them empty.

Then the priest, at my desire, brought me to one of the temples, that I might seek out all things concerning Herodotus the Halicarnassian, from one who knew. Now this temple is not the fairest in the city, but less fair and goodly than the old temples, yet goodlier and more fair than the new temples; and over the roof there is the image of an eagle made of stone—no small marvel, but a great one, how men came to fashion him; and that temple is called the House of Queens. Here they sacrifice a boar once every year; and concerning this they tell a certain sacred story which I know but will not utter.

Then I was brought to the priest who had a name for knowing most about Egypt, and the Egyptians, and the Assyrians, and the Cappadocians, and all the kingdoms of the Great King. He came out to me, being attired in a black robe, and wearing on his head a square cap. But why the priests have square caps I know, and he who has been initiated into the mysteries which they call 'Matric' knows, but I prefer not to tell. Concerning the square cap, then, let this be sufficient. Now, the priest received me courteously, and when I asked him, concerning Herodotus, whether he were a true man or not, he smiled, and answered 'Abu Goosh,' which, in the tongue of the Arabians, means 'The Father of Liars.' Then he went on to speak concerning Herodotus, and he said in his discourse that Herodotus not only told the thing which was not, but that he did so wilfully, as one knowing the truth but concealing it. For example, quoth he, 'Solon never went to see Croesus, as Herodotus avers; nor did those about Xerxes ever dream dreams; but Herodotus, out of his abundant wickedness, invented these things.

'Now behold,' he went on, 'how the curse of the Gods falls upon Herodotus. For he pretends that he saw Cadmeian inscriptions at Thebes. Now I do not believe there were any Cadmeian inscriptions there: therefore Herodotus is most manifestly lying. Moreover, this Herodotus never speaks of Sophocles the Athenian, and why not? Because he, being a child at school, did not learn Sophocles by heart: for the tragedies of Sophocles could not have been learned at school before they were written, nor can any man quote a poet whom he never learned at school. Moreover, as all those about Herodotus knew Sophocles well, he could not appear to them to be learned by showing that he knew what they knew also.' Then I thought the priest was making game and sport, saying first that Herodotus could know no poet whom he had not learned at school, and then saying that all the men of his time well knew this poet, 'about whom everyone was talking'. But the priest seemed not to know that Herodotus and Sophocles were friends, which is proved by this, that Sophocles wrote an ode in praise of Herodotus.

Then he went on, and though I were to write with a hundred hands (like Briareus, of whom Homer makes mention) I could not tell you all the things that the priest said against Herodotus, speaking truly, or not truly, or sometimes correctly and sometimes not, as often befalls mortal men. For Herodotus, he said, was chiefly concerned to steal the lore of those who came before him, such as Hecataeus, and then to escape notice as having stolen it. Also he said that, being himself cunning and deceitful, Herodotus was easily beguiled by the cunning of others, and believed in things manifestly false, such as the story of the Phoenix-bird.

23

Then I spoke, and said that Herodotus himself declared that he could not believe that story; but the priest regarded me not. And he said that Herodotus had never caught a crocodile with cold pig, nor did he ever visit Assyria, nor Babylon, nor Elephantine; but, saying that he had been in these lands, said that which was not true. He also declared that Herodotus, when he travelled, knew none of the Fat Ones of the Egyptians, but only those of the baser sort. And he called Herodotus a thief and a beguiler, and 'the same with intent to deceive,' as one of their own poets writes, and, to be short, Herodotus, I could not tell you in one day all the charges which are now brought against you; but concerning the truth of these things, you know, not least, but most, as to yourself being guilty or innocent. Wherefore, if you have anything to show or set forth whereby you may be relieved from the burden of these accusations, now is the time. Be no more silent; but, whether through the Oracle of the Dead, or the Oracle of Branchidae, or that in Delphi, or Dodona, or of Amphiaraus at Oropus, speak to your friends and lovers (whereof I am one from of old) and let men know the very truth.

Now, concerning the priests in the City of the Ford of the Ox, it is to be said that of all men whom we know they receive strangers most gladly, feasting them all day. Moreover, they have many drinks, cunningly mixed, and of these the best is that they call Archdeacon, naming it from one of the priests' offices. Truly, as Homer says (if the Odyssey be Homer's), 'when that draught is poured into the bowl then it is no pleasure to refrain.'

Drinking of this wine, or nectar, Herodotus, I pledge you, and pour forth some deal on the ground, to Herodotus of Halicarnassus, in the House of Hades.

24

And I wish you farewell, and good be with you. Whether the priest spoke truly, or not truly, even so may such good things betide you as befall dead men.

V

Epistle to Mr. Alexander Pope

From mortal Gratitude, decide, my Pope,
Have Wits Immortal more to fear or hope?
Wits toil and travail round the Plant of Fame,
Their Works its Garden, and its Growth their Aim,
Then Commentators, in unwieldy Dance,
Break down the Barriers of the trim Pleasance,
Pursue the Poet, like Actaeon's Hounds,
Beyond the fences of his Garden Grounds,
Rend from the singing Robes each borrowed gem,
Rend from the laurel'd Brows the Diadem,
And, if one Rag of Character they spare,
Comes the Biographer, and strips it bare!

Such, Pope, has been thy Fortune, such thy Doom.
Swift the Ghouls gathered at the Poet's Tomb,
With Dust of Notes to clog each lordly Line,
Warburton, Warton, Croker, Bowles, combine!
Collecting Cackle, Johnson condescends
To interview the Drudges of your Friends.
Though still your Courthope holds your merits high,
And still proclaims your Poems poetry,
Biographers, un-Boswell-like, have sneered,
And Dunces edit him whom Dunces feared!

They say; what say they? Not in vain You ask.
To tell you what they say, behold my Task!
'Methinks already I your Tears survey'
As I repeat 'the horrid Things they say.'[2]

Comes El—n first: I fancy you'll agree
Not frenzied Dennis smote so fell as he;
For El—n's Introduction, crabbed and dry,
Like Churchill's Cudgel's[3] marked with Lie, and Lie!

'Too dull to know what his own System meant,
Pope yet was skilled new Treasons to invent;
A Snake that puffed himself and stung his Friends,
Few Lied so frequent, for such little Ends;
His mind, like Flesh inflamed,[4] was raw and sore,
And still, the more he writhed, he stung the more!
Oft in a Quarrel, never in the Right,
His Spirit sank when he was called to fight.
Pope, in the Darkness mining like a Mole,
Forged on Himself, as from Himself he stole,
And what for Caryll once he feigned to feel,
Transferred, in Letters never sent, to Steele!
Still he denied the Letters he had writ,
And still mistook Indecency for Wit.
His very Grammar, so De Quincey cries,
"Detains the Reader, and at times defies!"'

Fierce El—n thus: no Line escapes his Rage,

---

² Rape of the Lock
³ In Mr Hogarth's Caricatura
⁴ Elwyn's Pope, ii. 15

27

And furious Foot-notes growl 'neath every Page:
See St-ph-n next take up the woful Tale,
Prolong the Preaching, and protract the Wail!
'Some forage Falsehoods from the North and South,
But Pope, poor D—-l, lied from Hand to Mouth;[5]
Affected, hypocritical, and vain,
A Book in Breeches, and a Fop in Grain;
A Fox that found not the high Clusters sour,
The Fanfaron of Vice beyond his power,
Pope yet possessed'—(the Praise will make you start)—
'Mean, morbid, vain, he yet possessed a Heart!
And still we marvel at the Man, and still
Admire his Finish, and applaud his Skill:
Though, as that fabled Barque, a phantom Form,
Eternal strains, nor rounds the Cape of Storm,
Even so Pope strove, nor ever crossed the Line
That from the Noble separates the Fine!'

The Learned thus, and who can quite reply,
Reverse the Judgment, and Retort the Lie?
You reap, in arméd Hates that haunt Your name,
Reap what you sowed, the Dragon's Teeth of Fame:
You could not write, and from unenvious Time
Expect the Wreath that crowns the lofty Rhyme,
You still must fight, retreat, attack, defend,
And oft, to snatch a Laurel, lose a Friend!

The Pity of it! And the changing Taste

---

[5] 'Poor Pope was always a hand-to-mouth liar.'
—Pope, by Leslie Stephen, 139

Of changing Time leaves half your Work a Waste!
My Childhood fled your couplet's clarion tone,
And sought for Homer in the Prose of Bohn.
Still through the Dust of that dim Prose appears
The Flight of Arrows and the Sheen of Spears;
Still we may trace what Hearts heroic feel,
And hear the Bronze that hurtles on the Steel!
But, ah, your Iliad seems a half-pretence,
Where Wits, not Heroes, prove their Skill in Fence,
And great Achilles' Eloquence doth show
As if no Centaur trained him, but Boileau!
Again, your Verse is orderly,—and more,—
'The Waves behind impel the Waves before;'
Monotonously musical they glide,
Till Couplet unto Couplet hath replied.
But turn to Homer! How his Verses sweep!
Surge answers Surge and Deep doth call on Deep;
This Line in Foam and Thunder issues forth,
Spurred by the West or smitten by the North,
Sombre in all its sullen Deeps, and all
Clear at the Crest, and foaming to the Fall,
The next with silver Murmur dies away,
Like Tides that falter to Calypso's Bay!

Thus Time, with sordid Alchemy and dread,
Turns half the Glory of your Gold to Lead;
Thus Time,—at Ronsard's wreath that vainly bit,—
Has marred the Poet to preserve the Wit,
Who almost left on Addison a stain,
Whose knife cut cleanest with a poisoned pain,—
Yet Thou (strange Fate that clings to all of Thine!)

When most a Wit dost most a Poet shine.
In Poetry thy Dunciad expires,
When Wit has shot 'her momentary Fires.'
'T is Tragedy that watches by the Bed
'Where tawdry Yellow strove with dirty Red,'
And men, remembering all, can scarce deny
To lay the Laurel where thine Ashes lie!

VI

To Lucian of Samosata

In what bower, oh Lucian, of your rediscovered Islands Fortunate are you now reclining; the delight of the fair, the learned, the witty, and the brave? In that clear and tranquil climate, whose air breathes of 'violet and lily, myrtle, and the flower of the vine,'

> *Where the daisies are rose-scented,*
> *And the Rose herself has got*
> *Perfume which on earth is not,*

among the music of all birds, and the wind-blown notes of flutes hanging on the trees, methinks that your laughter sounds most silvery sweet, and that Helen and fair Charmides are still of your company. Master of mirth, and Soul the best contented of all that have seen the world's ways clearly, most clear-sighted of all that have made tranquillity their bride, what other laughers dwell with you, where the crystal and fragrant waters wander round the shining palaces and the temples of amethyst?

Heine surely is with you; if, indeed, it was not one Syrian soul that dwelt among alien men, Germans and Romans, in the bodily tabernacles of Heine and of Lucian. But he was fallen on evil times and evil tongues; while Lucian, as witty as he, as bitter in mockery, as happily dowered with the magic of words, lived long and happily and honoured, imprisoned in no 'mattress-grave.' Without Rabelais, without Voltaire, without Heine, you would find, methinks, even the joys of your Happy Islands lacking in zest; and, unless Plato came by your way, none of the ancients could meet you in the lists of sportive dialogue.

There, among the vines that bear twelve times in the year, more excellent than all the vineyards of Touraine, while the song-birds bring you flowers from vales enchanted, and the shapes of the Blessed come and go, beautiful in wind-woven raiment of sunset hues; there, in a land that knows not age nor winter, midnight, nor autumn, nor noon, where the silver twilight of summer-dawn is perennial, where youth does not wax spectre-pale and die; there, my Lucian, you are crowned the Prince of the Paradise of Mirth.

Who would bring you, if he had the power, from the banquet where Homer sings: Homer, who, in mockery of commentators, past and to come, German and Greek, informed you that he was by birth a Babylonian? Yet, if you, who first wrote Dialogues of the Dead, could hear the prayer of an epistle wafted to 'lands indiscoverable in the unheard-of West,' you might visit once more a world so worthy of such a mocker, so like the world you knew so well of old.

Ah, Lucian, we have need of you, of your sense and of your mockery! Here, where faith is sick and superstition is waking afresh; where gods come rarely, and spectres appear at five shillings an interview; where science is popular, and philosophy cries aloud in the market-place, and clamour does duty for government, and Thais and Lais are names of power—here, Lucian, is room and scope for you. Can I not imagine a new 'Auction of Philosophers,' and what wealth might be made by him who bought these popular sages and lecturers at his estimate, and vended them at their own?

HERMES: Whom shall we put first up to auction?

ZEUS: That German in spectacles; he seems a highly respectable man.

HERMES: Ho, pessimist, come down and let the public view you.

ZEUS: Go on, put him up and have done with him.

HERMES: Who bids for the Life Miserable, for extreme, complete, perfect, unredeemable perdition? What offers for the universal extinction of the species, and the collapse of the Conscious?

A PURCHASER: He does not look at all a bad lot. May one put him through his paces?

HERMES: Certainly; try your luck.

PURCHASER: What is your name?

PESSIMIST: Hartmann.

PURCHASER: What can you teach me?

PESSIMIST: That Life is not worth Living.

PURCHASER: Wonderful! Most edifying! How much for this lot?

HERMES: Two hundred pounds.

PURCHASER: I will write you a cheque for the money. Come home, Pessimist, and begin your lessons without more ado.

HERMES: Attention! Here is a magnificent article—the Positive Life, the Scientific Life, the Enthusiastic Life. Who bids for a possible place in the Calendar of the Future?

PURCHASER: What does he call himself? he has a very French air.

HERMES: Put your own questions.

33

PURCHASER: What's your pedigree, my Philosopher, and previous performances?

POSITIVIST: I am by Rousseau out of Catholicism, with a strain of the Evolution blood.

PURCHASER: What do you believe in?

POSITIVIST: In Man, with a large M.

PURCHASER: Not in individual Man?

POSITIVIST: By no means; not even always in Mr. Gladstone. All men, all Churches, all parties, all philosophies, and even the other sect of our own Church, are perpetually in the wrong. Buy me, and listen to me, and you will ahvays be in the right.

PURCHASER: And, after this life, what have you to offer me?

POSITIVIST: A distinguished position in the Choir Invisible: but not, of course, conscious immortality.

PURCHASER: Take him away, and put up another lot.

Then the Hegelian, with his Notion, and the Darwinian, with his notions, and the Lotzian, with his Broad Church mixture of Religion and Evolution, and the Spencerian, with that Absolute which is a sort of a something, might all be offered with their divers wares; and cheaply enough, Lucian, you would value them in this auction of Sects. 'There is but one way to Corinth,' as of old; but which that way may be, oh master of Hermotimus, we know no more than he did of old; and still we find, of all philosophies, that the Stoic route is most to be recommended. But we have our Cyrenaics too, though they are no longer 'clothed in purple, and crowned with flowers, and fond of drink and of female flute-

34

players.' Ah, here too, you might laugh, and fail to see where the Pleasure lies, when the Cyrenaics are no 'judges of cakes' (nor of ale, for that matter), and are strangers in the Courts of Princes. 'To despise all things, to make use of all things, in all things to follow pleasure only:' that is not the manner of the new, if it were the secret of the older Hedonism.

Then, turning from the philosophers to the seekers after a sign, what change, Lucian, would you find in them and their ways? None; they are quite unaltered. Still our Perigrinus, and our Perigrina too, come to us from the East, or, if from the West, they take India on their way—India, that secular home of drivelling creeds, and of religion in its sacerdotage. Still they prattle of Brahmins and Buddhism; though, unlike Peregrinus, they do not publicly burn themselves on pyres, at Epsom Downs, after the Derby. We are not so fortunate in the demise of our Theosophists; and our police, less wise than the Hellenodicae, would probably not permit the Immolation of the Quack. Like your Alexander, they deal in marvels and miracles, oracles and warnings. All such bogy stories as those of your 'Philopseudes,' and the ghost of the lady who took to table-rapping because one of her best slippers had not been burned with her body, are gravely investigated by the Psychical Society.

Even your ignorant Bibliophile is still with us—the man without a tinge of letters, who buys up old manuscripts 'because they are stained and gnawed, and who goes, for proof of valued antiquity, to the testimony of the book-worms.' And the rich Bibliophile now, as in your satire, clothes his volumes in purple morocco and gay dorures, while their contents are sealed to him.

As to the topics of satire and gay curiosity which occupy the lady known as 'Gyp,' and M. Halévy in his 'Les Petites Cardinal,' if you had not exhausted the matter in your 'Dialogues of Hetairai,' you would be amused to find the same old traits surviving without a touch of change. One reads, in Halévy's French, of Madame Cardinal, and, in your Greek, of the mother of Philinna, and marvels that eighteen hundred years have not in one single trifle altered the mould. Still the old shabby light-loves, the old greed, the old luxury and squalor. Still the unconquerable superstition that now seeks to tell fortunes by the cards, and, in your time, resorted to the sorceress with her magical 'bull-roarer' or 'turndun.'[6]

Yes, Lucian, we are the same vain creatures of doubt and dread, of unbelief and credulity, of avarice and pretence, that you knew, and at whom you smiled. Nay, our very 'social question' is not altered. Do you not write, in 'The Runaways,' 'The artisans will abandon their workshops, and leave their trades, when they see that, with all the labour that bows their bodies from dawn to dark, they make a petty and starveling pittance, while men that toil not nor spin are floating in Pactolus'?

They begin to see this again as of yore; but whether the end of their vision will be a laughing matter, you, fortunate Lucian, do not need to care. Hail to you, and farewell!

---

[6] The Greek rombos [transliterated], mentioned by Lucian and Theocritus, was the magical weapon of the Australians— the turndun.

VII

To Maitre Francoys Rabelais

Of the Coming of the Coqcigrues

Master,—In the Boreal and Septentrional lands, turned aside from the noonday and the sun, there dwelt of old (as thou knowest, and as Olaus voucheth) a race of men, brave, strong, nimble, and adventurous, who had no other care but to fight and drink. There, by reason of the cold (as Virgil witnesseth), men break wine with axes. To their minds, when once they were dead and gotten to Valhalla, or the place of their Gods, there would be no other pleasure but to swig, tipple, drink, and boose till the coming of that last darkness and Twilight, wherein they, with their deities, should do battle against the enemies of all mankind; which day they rather desired than dreaded.

So chanced it also with Pantagruel and Brother John and their company, after they had once partaken of the secret of the Dive Bouteille. Thereafter they searched no longer; but, abiding at their ease, were merry, frolic, jolly, gay, glad, and wise; only that they always and ever did expect the awful Coming of the Coqcigrues. Now concerning the day of that coming, and the nature of them that should come, they knew nothing; and for his part Panurge was all the more adread, as Aristotle testifieth that men (and Panurge above others) most fear that which they know least. Now it chanced one day, as they sat at meat, with viands rare, dainty, and precious

37

as ever Apicius dreamed of, that there fluttered on the air a faint sound as of sermons, speeches, orations, addresses, discourses, lectures, and the like; whereat Panurge, pricking up his ears, cried, 'Methinks this wind bloweth from Midlothian,' and so fell a trembling.

Next, to their aural orifices, and the avenues audient of the brain, was borne a very melancholy sound as of harmoniums, hymns, organ-pianos, psalteries, and the like, all playing different airs, in a kind most hateful to the Muses. Then said Panurge, as well as he might for the chattering of his teeth: 'May I never drink if here come not the Coqcigrues!' and this saying and prophecy of his was true and inspired. But thereon the others began to mock, flout, and gird at Panurge for his cowardice. 'Here am I!' cried Brother John, 'well-armed and ready to stand a siege; being entrenched, fortified, hemmed-in and surrounded with great pasties, huge pieces of salted beef, salads, fricassees, hams, tongues, pies, and a wilderness of pleasant little tarts, jellies, pastries, trifles, and fruits of all kinds, and I shall not thirst while I have good wells, founts, springs, and sources of Bordeaux wine, Burgundy, wine of the Champagne country, sack and Canary. A fig for thy Coqcigrues!'

But even as he spoke there ran up suddenly a whole legion, or rather army, of physicians, each armed with laryngoscopes, stethoscopes, horoscopes, microscopes, weighing machines, and such other tools, engines, and arms as they had who, after thy time, persecuted Monsieur de Pourceaugnac! And they all, rushing on Brother John, cried out to him, 'Abstain! Abstain!' And one said, 'I have well diagnosed thee, and thou art in a fair way to have the gout.' 'I never did better in my days,' said Brother John. 'Away with thy meats and drinks!' they cried. And one said, 'He must to Royat;' and another, 'Hence with him to Aix;' and a third, 'Banish him to

Wiesbaden;' and a fourth, 'Hale him to Gastein;' and yet another, 'To Barbouille with him in chains!'

And while others felt his pulse and looked at his tongue, they all wrote prescriptions for him like men mad. 'For thy eating,' cried he that seemed to be their leader, 'No soup!' 'No soup!' quoth Brother John; and those cheeks of his, whereat you might have warmed your two hands in the winter solstice, grew white as lilies. 'Nay! and no salmon nor any beef nor mutton! A little chicken by times, but periculo tuo! Nor any game, such as grouse, partridge, pheasant, capercailzie, wild duck; nor any cheese, nor fruit, nor pastry, nor coffee, nor eau de vie; and avoid all sweets. No veal, pork, nor made dishes of any kind.' 'Then what may I eat?' quoth the good Brother, whose valour had oozed out of the soles of his sandals. 'A little cold bacon at breakfast—no eggs,' quoth the leader of the strange folk, 'and a slice of toast without butter.' 'And for thy drink'—('What?' gasped Brother John)—'one dessert-spoonful of whisky, with a pint of the water of Apollinaris at luncheon and dinner. No more!' At this Brother John fainted, falling like a great buttress of a hill, such as Taygetus or Erymanthus.

While they were busy with him, others of the frantic folk had built great platforms of wood, whereon they all stood and spoke at once, both men and women. And of these some wore red crosses on their garments, which meaneth 'Salvation;' and others wore white crosses, with a little black button of crape, to signify 'Purity;' and others bits of blue to mean 'Abstinence.' While some of these pursued Panurge others did beset Pantagruel; asking him very long questions, whereunto he gave but short answers. Thus they asked:

Have ye Local Option here?—Pan.: What?

May one man drink if his neighbour be not athirst?—Pan.: Yea!

Have ye Free Education?—Pan.: What?

Must they that have, pay to school them that have not?—Pan.: Nay

Have ye free land?—Pan.: What?

Have ye taken the land from the farmer, and given it to the tailor out of work and the candlemaker masterless?—Pan.: Nay!

Have your women folk votes?—Pan.: Bosh!

Have ye got religion?—Pan.: How?

Do you go about the streets at night, brawling, blowing a trumpet before you, and making long prayers?—Pan.: Nay

Have you manhood suffrage?—Pan.: Eh?

Is Jack as good as his master? Pan.: Nay!

Have you joined the Arbitration Society?—Pan.: Quoy??

Will you let another kick you, and will you ask his neighbour if you deserve the same?—Pan.: Nay?

Do you cat what you list?—Pan.: Ay!

Do you drink when you are athirst? Pan.: Ay!

Are you governed by the free expression of the popular will?—Pan.: How?

Are you servants of priests, pulpits, and penny papers?—Pan.: No!

Now, when they heard these answers of Pantagruel they all fell, some a weeping, some a praying, some a swearing, some an arbitrating, some a lecturing, some a caucussing, some a preaching,

40

some a faith-healing, some a miracle-working, some a hypnotising, some a writing to the daily press; and while they were thus busy, like folk distraught, 'reforming the island,' Pantagruel burst out a laughing; whereat they were greatly dismayed; for laughter killeth the whole race of Coqcigrues, and they may not endure it.

Then Pantagruel and his company stole aboard a barque that Panurge had ready in the harbour. And having provisioned her well with store of meat and good drink, they set sail for the kingdom of Entelechy, where, having landed, they were kindly entreated; and there abide to this day; drinking of the sweet and eating of the fat, under the protection of that intellectual sphere which hath in all places its centre and nowhere its circumference.

Such was their destiny; there was their end appointed, and thither the Coqcigrues can never come. For all the air of that land is full of laughter, which killeth Coqcigrues; and there aboundeth the herb Pantagruelion. But for thee, Master Francoys, thou art not well liked in this island of ours, where the Coqcigrues are abundant, very fierce, cruel, and tyrannical. Yet thou hast thy friends, that meet and drink to thee and wish thee well wheresoever thou hast found thy grand peut-étre.

41

VIII

To Jane Austen

Madame,—If to the enjoyments of your present state be lacking a view of the minor infirmities or foibles of men, I cannot but think (were the thought permitted) that your pleasures are yet incomplete. Moreover, it is certain that a woman of parts who has once meddled with literature will never wholly lose her love for the discussion of that delicious topic, nor cease to relish what (in the cant of our new age) is styled 'literary shop.' For these reasons I attempt to convey to you some inkling of the present state of that agreeable art which you, madam, raised to its highest pitch of perfection.

As to your own works (immortal, as I believe), I have but little that is wholly cheering to tell one who, among women of letters, was almost alone in her freedom from a lettered vanity. You are not a very popular author: your volumes are not found in gaudy covers on every bookstall; or, if found, are not perused with avidity by the Emmas and Catherines of our generation. 'Tis not long since a blow was dealt (in the estimation of the unreasoning) at your character as an author by the publication of your familiar letters. The editor of these epistles, unfortunately, did not always take your witticisms, and he added others which were too unmistakably his own. While the injudicious were disappointed by the absence of your exquisite style and humour, the wiser sort were the more convinced of your wisdom. In your letters (knowing your correspondents) you gave but the small personal talk of the hour, for them sufficient; for your books you reserved matter and expression which are imperishable. Your admirers, if not very numerous, include all persons of taste, who, in your favour, are apt somewhat to abate the rule, or shake off the habit, which commonly confines them to but temperate laudation.

'T is the fault of all art to seem antiquated and faded in the eyes of the succeeding generation. The manners of your age were not the manners of to-day, and young gentlemen and ladies who think Scott 'slow,' think Miss Austen 'prim' and 'dreary.' Yet, even could you return among us, I scarcely believe that, speaking the language of the hour, as you might, and versed in its habits, you would win the general admiration. For how tame, madam, are your characters, especially your favourite heroines! how limited the life which you knew and described! how narrow the range of your incidents! how correct your grammar!

As heroines, for example, you chose ladies like Emma, and Elizabeth, and Catherine: women remarkable neither for the brilliance nor for the degradation of their birth; women wrapped up in their own and the parish's concerns, ignorant of evil, as it seems, and unacquainted with vain yearnings and interesting doubts. Who can engage his fancy with their match-makings and the conduct of their affections, when so many daring and dazzling heroines approach and solicit his regard?

Here are princesses dressed in white velvet stamped with golden fleurs-de-lys—ladies with hearts of ice and lips of fire, who count their roubles by the million, their lovers by the score, and even their husbands, very often, in figures of some arithmetical importance. With these are the immaculate daughters of itinerant Italian musicians, maids whose souls are unsoiled amidst the contaminations of our streets, and whose acquaintance with the art of Phidias and Praxiteles, of Daedalus and Scopas, is the more admirable, because entirely derived from loving study of the inexpensive collections vended by the plaster-of-Paris man round the corner. When such heroines are wooed by the nephews of Dukes, where are your Emmas and Elizabeths? Your volumes neither excite nor satisfy the curiosities provoked by that modern and scientific fiction, which is greatly admired, I learn, in the United States, as well as in France and at home.

You erred, it cannot be denied, with your eyes open. Knowing Lydia and Kitty so intimately as you did, why did you make of them almost insignificant characters? With Lydia for a heroine you might have gone far; and, had you devoted three volumes, and the chief of your time, to the passions of Kitty, you might have held your own, even now, in the circulating library. How Lyddy, perched on a corner of the roof, first beheld her Wickham; how, on her challenge, he climbed up by a ladder to her side; how they kissed, caressed, swung on gates together, met at odd seasons, in strange places, and finally eloped: all this might have been put in the mouth of a jealous elder sister, say Elizabeth, and you would not have been less popular than several favourites of our time. Had you cast the whole narrative into the present tense, and lingered lovingly over the thickness of Mary's legs and the softness of Kitty's cheeks, and the blonde fluffiness of Wickham's whiskers, you would have left a romance still dear to young ladies.

Or again, you might entrance your students still, had you concentrated your attention on Mrs. Rushworth, who eloped with Henry Crawford. These should have been the chief figures of 'Mansfield Park.' But you timidly decline to tackle Passion. 'Let other pens,' you write, 'dwell on guilt and misery. I quit such

44

odious subjects as soon as I can.' Ah, there is the secret of your failure! Need I add that the vulgarity and narrowness of the social circles you describe impair your popularity? I scarce remember more than one lady of title, and but very few lords (and these unessential) in all your tales. Now, when we all wish to be in society, we demand plenty of titles in our novels, at any rate, and we get lords (and very queer lords) even from Republican authors, born in a country which in your time was not renowned for its literature. I have heard a critic remark, with a decided air of fashion, on the brevity of the notice which your characters give each other when they offer invitations to dinner. 'An invitation to dinner next day was despatched,' and this demonstrates that your acquaintance 'went out' very little, and had but few engagements. How vulgar, too, is one of your heroines, who bids Mr. Darcy 'keep his breath to cool his porridge.' I blush for Elizabeth! It were superfluous to add that your characters are debased by being invariably mere members of the Church of England as by law established. The Dissenting enthusiast, the open soul that glides from Esoteric Buddhism to the Salvation Army, and from the Higher Pantheism to the Higher Paganism, we look for in vain among your studies of character. Nay, the very words I employ are of unknown sound to you; so how can you help us in the stress of the soul's travailings?

You may say that the soul's travailings are no affair of yours; proving thereby that you have indeed but a lowly conception of the duty of the novelist. I only remember one reference, in all your works, to that controversy which occupies the chief of our attention—the great controversy on Creation or Evolution. Your Jane Bennet cries: 'I have no idea of there being so much Design in the world as some persons imagine.' Nor do you touch on our

45

mighty social question, the Land Laws, save when Mrs. Bennet appears as a Land Reformer, and rails bitterly against the cruelty 'of settling an estate away from a family of five daughters, in favour of a man whom nobody cared anything about.' There, madam, in that cruelly unjust performance, what a text you had for a Tendenz-Roman. Nay, you can allow Kitty to report that a Private had been flogged, without introducing a chapter on Flogging in the Army. But you formally declined to stretch your matter out, here and there, 'with solemn specious nonsense about something unconnected with the story.' No 'padding' for Miss Austen! In fact, madam, as you were born before Analysis came in, or Passion, or Realism, or Naturalism, or Irreverence, or Religious Open-mindedness, you really cannot hope to rival your literary sisters in the minds of a perplexed generation. Your heroines are not passionate, we do not see their red wet cheeks, and tresses dishevelled in the manner of our frank young Maenads. What says your best successor, a lady who adds fresh lustre to a name that in fiction equals yours? She says of Miss Austen: 'Her heroines have a stamp of their own. They have a certain gentle self-respect and humour and hardness of heart... Love with them does not mean a passion as much as an interest, deep and silent.' I think one prefers them so, and that Englishwomen should be more like Anne Elliot than Maggie Tulliver. 'All the privilege I claim for my own sex is that of loving longest when existence or when hope is gone,' said Anne; perhaps she insisted on a monopoly that neither sex has all to itself. Ah, madam, what a relief it is to come back to your witty volumes, and forget the follies of to-day in those of Mr. Collins and of Mrs. Bennet! How fine, nay, how noble is your art in its delicate reserve, never insisting, never forcing the note, never pushing the sketch into the caricature! You worked without thinking of it, in the spirit of Greece, on a labour happily limited, and exquisitely organised. 'Dear books,' we say, with Miss Thackeray—'dear books, bright, sparkling with wit and animation, in which the homely heroines charm, the dull hours fly, and the very bores are enchanting.'

IX

To Master Isaak Walton

Father Isaak,—When I would be quiet and go angling it is my custom to carry in my wallet thy pretty book, 'The Compleat Angler.' Here, methinks, if I find not trout I shall find content, and good company, and sweet songs, fair milkmaids, and country mirth. For you are to know that trout be now scarce, and whereas he was ever a fearful fish, he hath of late become so wary that none but the cunningest anglers may be even with him.

It is not as it was in your time, Father, when a man might leave his shop in Fleet Street, of a holiday, and, when he had stretched his legs up Tottenham Hill, come lightly to meadows chequered with waterlilies and lady-smocks, and so fall to his sport. Nay, now have the houses so much increased, like a spreading sore (through the breaking of that excellent law of the Conscientious King and blessed Martyr, whereby building beyond the walls was forbidden), that the meadows are all swallowed up in streets. And as to the River Lea, wherein you took many a good trout, I read in the news sheets that 'its bed is many inches thick in horrible filth, and the air for more than half a mile on each side of it is polluted with a horrible, sickening stench,' so that we stand in dread of a new Plague, called the Cholera. And so it is all about London for many miles, and if a man, at heavy charges, betake himself to the fields, lo you, folk are grown so greedy that none will suffer a stranger to fish in his water.

So poor anglers are in sore straits. Unless a man be rich and can pay great rents, he may not fish, in England, and hence spring the discontents of the times, for the angler is full of content, if he do but take trout, but if he be driven from the waterside, he falls, perchance, into evil company, and cries out to divide the property of the gentle folk. As many now do, even among Parliament, men, whom you loved not, Father Isaak, neither do I love them more than Reason and Scripture bid each of us be kindly to his neighbour. But, behold, the causes of the ill content are not yet all expressed, for even where a man hath licence to fish, he will hardly take trout in our age, unless he be all the more cunning. For the fish, harried this way and that by so many of your disciples, is exceeding shy and artful, nor will he bite at a fly unless it falleth lightly, just above his mouth, and floateth dry over him, for all the world like the natural ephemeris. And we may no longer angle with worm for him, nor with penk or minnow, nor with the natural fly, as was your manner, but only with the artificial, for the more difficulty the more diversion. For my part I may cry, like Viator in your book, 'Master, I can neither catch with the first nor second Angle: I have no fortune.'

So we fare in England, but somewhat better north of the Tweed, where trout are less wary, but for the most part small, except in the extreme rough north, among horrid hills and lakes. Thither, Master, as methinks you may remember, went Richard Franck, that called himself Philanthropus, and was, as it were, the Columbus of anglers, discovering for them a new Hyperborean world. But Franck, doubtless, is now an angler in the Lake of Darkness, with Nero and other tyrants, for he followed after Cromwell, the man of blood, in the old riding days. How wickedly doth Franck boast of that leader of the giddy multitude, 'when they raged, and became restless to find out misery for themselves and others, and the rabble would herd themselves together,' as you said, 'and endeavour to govern and act in spite of authority.' So you wrote; and what said Franck, that recreant angler? Doth he not praise 'Ireton, Vane, Nevill, and Martin, and the most renowned, valorous, and victorious conqueror, Oliver Cromwell.' Natheless, with all his sins on his head, this Franck discovered Scotland for anglers, and my heart turns to him when he praises 'the glittering and resolute streams of Tweed.'

In those wilds of Assynt and Loch Rannoch, Father, we, thy followers, may yet take trout, and forget the evils of the times. But, to be done with Franck, how harshly he speaks of thee and thy book. 'For you may dedicate your opinion to what scribbling putationer you please; the Compleat Angler if you will, who tells you of a tedious fly story, extravagantly collected from antiquated authors, such as Gesner and Dubravius.' Again, he speaks of 'Isaac Walton, whose authority to me seems alike authentick, as is the general opinion of the vulgar prophet,' &c.

Certain I am that Franck, if a better angler than thou, was a worse man, who, writing his 'Dialogues Piscatorial' or 'Northern Memoirs' five years after the world welcomed thy 'Compleat Angler,' was jealous of thy favour with the people, and, may be, hated thee for thy loyalty and sound faith. But, Master, like a peaceful man avoiding contention, thou didst never answer this blustering Franck, but wentest quietly about thy quiet Lea, and left him his roaring Brora and windy Assynt. How could this noisy man know thee—and know thee he did, having argued with thee in Stafford— and not love Isaak Walton? A pedant angler, I call him, a plaguy angler, so let him huff away, and turn we to thee and to thy sweet charm in fishing for men.

How often, studying in thy book, have I hummed to myself that of Horace—

Laudis amore tumes? Sunt certa piacula quae te
Ter pure lecto poterunt recreare libello.

So healing a book for the frenzy of fame is thy discourse on meadows, and pure streams, and the country life. How peaceful, men say, and blessed must have been the life of this old man, how lapped in content, and hedged about by his own humility from the world! They forget, who speak thus, that thy years, which were many, were also evil, or would have seemed evil to divers that had tasted of thy fortunes. Thou wert poor, but that, to thee, was no sorrow, for greed of money was thy detestation. Thou wert of lowly rank, in an age when gentle blood was alone held in regard; yet tiny virtues made thee hosts of friends, and chiefly among religious men, bishops, and doctors of the Church. Thy private life was not unacquainted with sorrow; thy first wife and all her fair children were taken from thee like flowers in spring, though, in thine age, new love and new offspring comforted thee like 'the primrose of the later year.' Thy private griefs might have made thee bitter, or melancholy, so might the sorrows of the State and of the Church, which were deprived of their heads by cruel men, despoiled of their wealth, the pious driven, like thee, from their homes; fear everywhere, everywhere robbery and confusion: all this ruin might have angered another temper. But thou, Father, didst bear all with so much sweetness as perhaps neither natural temperament, nor a firm faith, nor the love of angling could alone have displayed. For we see many anglers (as witness Richard Franck aforesaid) who are angry men, and myself, when I get my hooks entangled at every cast in a tree, have come nigh to swear prophane.

Also we see religious men that are sour and fanatical, no rare thing

51

in the party that professes godliness. But neither private sorrow nor public grief could abate thy natural kindliness, nor shake a religion which was not untried, but had, indeed, passed through the furnace like fine gold. For if we find not Faith at all times easy, because of the oppositions of Science, and the searching curiosity of men's minds, neither was Faith a matter of course in thy day. For the learned and pious were greatly tossed about, like worthy Mr. Chillingworth, by doubts wavering between the Church of Rome and the Reformed Church of England. The humbler folk, also, were invited, now here, now there, by the clamours of fanatical Nonconformists, who gave themselves out to be somebody, while Atheism itself was not without many to witness to it. Therefore, such a religion as thine was not, so to say, a mere innocence of evil in the things of our Belief, but a reasonable and grounded faith, strong in despite of oppositions. Happy was the man in whom temper, and religion, and the love of the sweet country and an angler's pastime so conveniently combined; happy the long life which held in its hand that threefold clue through the labyrinth of human fortunes! Around thee Church and State might fall in ruins, and might be rebuilded, and thy tears would not be bitter, nor thy triumph cruel.

> *Thus, by God's blessing, it befell thee*
> *Nec turpem senectam*
> *Degere, nec cithara carentem.*

I would, Father, that I could get at the verity about thy poems. Those recommendatory verses with which thou didst grace the Lives of Dr. Donne and others of thy friends, redound more to the praise of thy kind heart than thy fancy. But what or whose was the pastoral poem of 'Thealma and Clearchus,' which thou didst set about printing in 1678, and gavest to the world in 1683? Thou

52

gavest John Chalkhill for the author's name, and a John Chalkhill of thy kindred died at Winchester, being eighty years of his age, in 1679. Now thou speakest of John Chalkhill as 'a friend of Edmund Spenser's,' and how could this be?

Are they right who hold that John Chalkhill was but a name of a friend, borrowed by thee out of modesty, and used as a cloak to cover poetry of thine own inditing? When Mr. Flatman writes of Chalkhill, 't is in words well fitted to thine own merit:

> Happy old man, whose worth all mankind knows
> Except himself, who charitably shows
> The ready road to virtue and to praise,
> The road to many long and happy days.

However it be, in that road, by quiet streams and through green pastures, thou didst walk all thine almost century of years, and we, who stray into thy path out of the highway of life, we seem to hold thy hand, and listen to thy cheerful voice. If our sport be worse, may our content be equal, and our praise, therefore, none the less. Father, if Master Stoddard, the great fisher of Tweed-side, be with thee, greet him for me, and thank him for those songs of his, and perchance he will troll thee a catch of our dear River.

> Tweed! winding and wild! where the heart is unbound,
> They know not, they dream not, who linger around,
> How the saddened will smile, and the wasted rewin
> From thee—the bliss withered within.

Or perhaps thou wilt better love,

> The lanesome Tala and the Lyne,
> And Mahon wi' its mountain rills,

53

An' Etterick, whose waters twine
Wi' Yarrow frae the forest hills;
An' Gala, too, and Teviot bright,
An' mony a stream o' playfu' speed,
Their kindred valleys a' unite
Amang the braes o' bonnie Tweed!

So, Master, may you sing against each other, you two good old anglers, like Peter and Corydon, that sang in your golden age.

X. To M. Chapelain.

Monsieur,—You were a popular writer, and an honourable, over-educated, upright gentleman. Of the latter character you can never be deprived, and I doubt not it stands you in better stead where you are, than the laurels which flourished so gaily, and faded so soon.

> *Laurel is green for a season, and Love is fair for a day,*
> *But Love grows bitter with treason, and laurel out-lives not May.*

I know not if Mr. Swinburne is correct in his botany, but your laurel certainly outlived not May, nor can we hope that you dwell where Orpheus and where Homer are. Some other crown, some other Paradise, we cannot doubt it, awaited un si bon homme. But the moral excellence that even Boileau admitted, ladfoi, l'honneur, la probiité, do not in Parnassus avail the popular poet, and some luckless Musset or Théophile, Regnier or Villars attains a kind of immortality denied to the man of many contemporary editions, and of a great commercial success.

If ever, for the confusion of Horace, any Poet was Made, you, Sir, should have been that fortunately manufactured article. You were, in matters of the Muses, the child of many prayers. Never, since Adam's day, have any parents but yours prayed for a poet-child. Then Destiny, that mocks the desires of men in general, and fathers in particular, heard the appeal, and presented M. Chapelain and Jeanne Corbiére his wife with the future author of 'La Pucelle.' Oh futile hopes of men, O pectora caeca! All was done that education could do for a genius which, among other qualities, 'especially lacked fire and imagination,' and an ear for verse—sad defects these in a child of the Muses. Your training in all the mechanics and metaphysics of criticism might have made you exclaim, like Rasselas, 'Enough! Thou hast convinced me that no human being can ever be a Poet.' Unhappily, you succeeded in convincing Cardinal Richelieu that to be a Poet was well within your powers, you received a pension of one thousand crowns, and were made Captain of the Cardinal's minstrels, as M. de Tréville was Captain of the King's Musketeers.

Ah, pleasant age to live in, when good intentions in poetry were more richly endowed than ever is Research, even Research in Prehistoric English, among us niggard moderns! How I wish I knew a Cardinal, or, even as you did, a Prime Minister, who would praise and pension me; but Envy be still! Your existence was more happy indeed; you constructed odes, corrected sonnets, presided at the Ho'tel Rambouillet, while the learned ladies were still young and fair, and you enjoyed a prodigious celebrity on the score of your yet unpublished Epic. 'Who, indeed,' says a sympathetic author, M. Théophile Gautier, 'who could expect less than a miracle from a man so deeply learned in the laws of art—a perfect Turk in the science of poetry, a person so well pensioned, and so favoured by the great?' Bishops and politicians combined in perfect good faith to advertise your merits. Hard must have been the heart that could resist the testimonials of your skill as a poet offered by the Duc de Montausier, and the learned Huet, Bishop of Avranches, and Monseigneur Godeau, Bishop of Vence, or M. Colbert, who had such a genius for finance.

If bishops and politicians and prime ministers skilled in finance, and some critics, Ménage and Sarrazin and Vaugetas, if ladies of birth and taste, if all the world in fact, combined to tell you that you were a great poet, how can we blame you for taking yourself seriously, and appraising yourself at the public estimate?

It was not in human nature to resist the evidence of the bishops especially, and when every minor poet believes in himself on the testimony of his own conceit, you may be acquitted of vanity if you listened to the plaudits of your friends. Nay, you ventured to pronounce judgment on contemporaries whom Posterity has preferred to your perfections. 'Moliére,' said you, 'understands the nature of comedy, and presents it in a natural style. The plot of his best pieces is borrowed, but not without judgment; his morale is fair, and he has only to avoid scurrility.'

Excellent, unconscious, popular Chapelain!

Of yourself you observed, in a Report on contemporary literature, that your 'courage and sincerity never allowed you to tolerate work not absolutely good.' And yet you regarded 'La Pucellé with some complacency.

On the 'Pucellé you were occupied during a generation of mortal men. I marvel not at the length of your labours, as you received a yearly pension till the Epic was finished, but your Muse was no Alcmena, and no Hercules was the result of that prolonged night of creations. First you gravely wrote out (it was the task of five years)

56

all the compositions in prose. Ah, why did you not leave it in that commonplace but appropriate medium? What says the Précieuse about you in Boileau's satire?

> *In Chapelain, for all his foes have said,*
> *She finds but one defect, he can't be read;*
> *Yet thinks the world might taste his maiden's woes,*
> *If only he would turn his verse to prose!*

The verse had been prose, and prose, perhaps, it should have remained. Yet for this precious 'Pucelle,' in the age when 'Paradise Lost' was sold for five pounds, you are believed to have received about four thousand. Horace was wrong, mediocre poets may exist (now and then), and he was a wise man who first spoke of aurea mediocritas. At length the great work was achieved, a work thrice blessed in its theme, that divine Maiden to whom France owes all, and whom you and Voltaire have recompensed so strangely. In folio, in italics, with a score of portraits and engravings, and culs de lampe, the great work was given to the world, and had a success. Six editions in eighteen months are figures which fill the poetic heart with envy and admiration. And then, alas! the bubble burst. A great lady, Madame de Longveille, hearing the 'Pucellé read aloud, murmured that it was 'perfect indeed, but perfectly wearisome.' Then the satires began, and the satirists never left you till your poetic reputation was a rag, till the mildest Abbé at Ménagés had his cheap sneer for Chapelain.

I make no doubt, Sir, that envy and jealousy had much to do with the onslaught on your 'Pucelle.' These qualities, alas! are not strange to literary minds; does not even Hesiod tell us 'potter hates potter, and poet hates poet'? But contemporary spites do not harm true genius. Who suffered more than Moliére from cabals? Yet neither

57

the court nor the town ever deserted him, and he is still the joy of the world. I admit that his adversaries were weaker than yours. What were Boursault and Le Boulanger, and Thomas Corneille and De Visé, what were they all compared to your enemy, Boileau? Brossette tells a story which really makes a man pity you. There was a M. de Puimorin who, to be in the fashion, laughed at your once popular Epic. 'It is all very well for a man to laugh who cannot even read.' Whereon M. de Puimorin replied: 'Qu'il n'avoit que trop su' lire, depuis que Chapelain s'étoit avisé de faire imprimer.' A new horror had been added to the accomplishment of reading since Chapelain had published. This repartee was applauded, and M. de Puimorin tried to turn it into an epigram. He did complete the last couplet,

> *Hélas! pour mes péchés, je n'ai su' que trop lire*
> *Depuis que tu fais imprimer.*

But by no labour would M. de Puimorin achieve the first two lines of his epigram. Then you remember what great allies came to his assistance. I almost blush to think that M. Despréaux, M. Racine, and M. de Moliére, the three most renowned wits of the time, conspired to complete the poor jest, and madden you. Well, bubble as your poetry was, you may be proud that it needed all these sharpest of pens to prick the bubble. Other poets, as popular as you, have been annihilated by an article. Macaulay puts forth his hand, and 'Satan Montgomery' was no more. It did not need a Macaulay, the laughter of a mob of little critics was enough to blow into space; but you probably have met Montgomery, and of contemporary failures or successes I do not speak.

I wonder, sometimes, whether the consensus of criticism ever made you doubt for a moment whether, after all, you were not a false child of Apollo? Was your complacency tortured, as the complacency of true poets has occasionally been, by doubts? Did you expect posterity to reverse the verdict of the satirists, and to do you justice? You answered your earliest assailant, Liniére, and, by a few changes of words, turned his epigrams into flattery. But I fancy, on the whole, you remained calm, unmoved, wrapped up in admiration of yourself. According to M. de Marivaux, who reviewed, as I am doing, the spirits of the mighty dead, you 'conceived, on the strength of your reputation, a great and serious veneration for yourself and your genius.' Probably you were protected by this invulnerable armour of an honest vanity, probably you declared that mere jealousy dictates the lines of Boileau, and that Chapelain's real fault was his popularity, and his pecuniary success, Qu'il soit le mieux renté de tous les beaux-esprits.

This, you would avow, was your offence, and perhaps you were not altogether mistaken. Yet posterity declines to read a line of yours, and, as we think of you, we are again set face to face with that eternal problem, how far is popularity a test of poetry? Burns was a poet, and popular. Byron was a popular poet, and the world agrees in the verdict of their own generation. But Montgomery, though he sold so well, was no poet, nor, Sir, I fear, was your verse made of the stuff of immortality. Criticism cannot hurt what is truly great; the Cardinal and the Academy left Chiméne as fair as ever, and as adorable. It is only pinchbeck that perishes under the acids of satire: gold defies them. Yet I sometimes ask myself, does the existence of popularity like yours justify the malignity of satire, which blesses neither him who gives, nor him who takes? Are poisoned arrows fair against a bad poet? I doubt it, Sir, holding that, even unpricked, a poetic bubble must soon burst by its own nature. Yet satire will assuredly be written so long as bad poets are

59

successful, and bad poets will assuredly reflect that their assailants are merely envious, and, while their vogue lasts, that Prime Ministers and the purchasing public are the only judges.

Monsieur,
Votre trés humble serviteur,
Andrew Lang.

60

XI

To Sir John Manndeville, Kt

(Of the Ways Into Ynde)

Sir John,—wit you well that men holden you but light, and some clepen you a Liar. And they say that you never were born in Englond, in the town of Seynt Albones, nor have seen and gone through manye diverse Londes. And there goeth an old knight at arms, and one that connes Latyn, and hath been beyond the sea, and hath seen Prester John's country. And he hath been in an Yle that men clepen Burmah, and there bin women bearded. Now men call him Colonel Henry Yule, and he hath writ of thee in his great booke, Sir John, and he holds thee but lightly. For he saith that ye did pill your tales out of Odoric his book, and that ye never saw snails with shells as big as houses, nor never met no Devyls, but part of that ye say, ye took it out of William of Boldensele his book, yet ye took not his wisdom, withal, but put in thine own foolishness. Nevertheless, Sir John, for the frailty of Mankynde, ye are held a good fellow, and a merry; so now, come, I shall tell you of the new ways into Ynde.

In that Lond they have a Queen that governeth all the Lond, and all they ben obeyssant to her. And she is the Queen of Englond; for Englishmen have taken all the Lond of Ynde. For they were right good werryoures of old, and wyse, noble, and worthy. But of late hath risen a new sort of Englishman very puny and fearful, and these men clepen Radicals. And they go ever in fear, and they scream on high for dread in the streets and the houses, and they fain would flee away from all that their fathers gat them with the sword. And this sort men call Scuttleres, but the mean folk and certain of the womenkind hear them gladly, and they say ever that Englishmen should flee out of Ynde. Fro England men gon to Ynde by many dyverse Contreyes. For Englishmen ben very stirring and nymble. For they ben in the seventh climate, that is of the Moon. And the Moon (ye have said it yourself, Sir John, natheless, is it true) is of lightly moving, for to go diverse ways, and see strange things, and other diversities of the Worlde. Wherefore Englishmen be lightly moving, and far wandering. And they gon to Ynde by the great Sea Ocean. First come they to Gibraltar, that was the point of Spain, and builded upon a rock; and there ben apes, and it is so strong that no man may take it. Natheless did Englishmen take it fro the Spanyard, and all to hold the way to Ynde. For ye may sail all about Africa, and past the Cape men clepen of Good Hope, but that way unto Ynde is long and the sea is weary. Wherefore men rather go by the Midland sea, and Englishmen have taken many Yles in that sea.

For first they have taken an Yle that is clept Malta; and therein built they great castles, to hold it against them of Fraunce, and Italy, and of Spain. And from this Ile of Malta Men gon to Cipre. And Cipre is right a good Yle, and a fair, and a great, and it hath 4 principal Cytees within him. And at Famagost is one of the principal Havens of the sea that is in the world, and Englishmen have but a lytel while gone won that Yle from the Sarazynes. Yet say that sort of Englishmen where of I told you, that is puny and sore adread, that the Lond is poisonous and barren and of no avail, for that Lond is much more hotter than it is here. Yet the Englishmen that ben werryoures dwell there in tents, and the skill is that they may ben the more fresh.

From Cypre, Men gon to the Lond of Egypte, and in a Day and a Night he that hath a good wind may come to the Haven of Alessandrie. Now the Lond of Egypt longeth to the Soudan, yet the Soudan longeth not to the Lond of Egypt. And when I say this, I do jape with words, and may hap ye understond me not. Now Englishmen went in shippes to Alessandrie, and brent it, and over ran the Lond, and their soudyours warred agen the Bedoynes, and all to hold the way to Ynde. For it is not long past since Frenchmen let dig a dyke, through the narrow spit of lond, from the Midland sea to the Red sea, wherein was Pharaoh drowned. So this is the shortest way to Ynde there may be, to sail through that dyke, if men gon by sea.

But all the Lond of Egypt is clepen the Vale enchaunted; for no man may do his business well that goes thither, but always fares he evil, and therefore clepen they Egypt the Vale perilous, and the sepulchre of reputations. And men say there that is one of the entrees of Helle. In that Vale is plentiful lack of Gold and Silver, for many misbelieving men, and many Christian men also, have gone often time for to take of the Thresoure that there was of old, and have pilled the Thresoure, wherefore there is none left. And Englishmen have let carry thither great store of our Thresoure, 9,000,000 of Pounds sterling, and whether they will see it agen I misdoubt me. For that Vale is alle fulle of Develes and Fiendes that men clepen Bondholderes, for that Egypt from of olde is the Lond of Bondage. And whatsoever Thresoure cometh into the Lond, these Devyls of Bondholders grabben the same. Natheless by that Vale do Englishmen go unto Ynde, and they gon by Aden, even to

Kurrachee, at the mouth of the Flood of Ynde. Thereby they send their souldyours, when they are adread of them of Muscovy.

For, look you, there is another way into Ynde, and thereby the men of Muscovy are fain to come, if the Englishmen let them not. That way cometh by Desert and Wildernesse, from the sea that is clept Caspian, even to Khiva, and so to Merv; and then come ye to Zulfikar and Penjdeh, and anon to Herat, that is called the Key of the Gates of Ynde. Then ye win the lond of the Emir of the Afghauns, a great prince and a rich, and he hath in his Thresoure more crosses, and stars, and coats that captains wearen, than any other man on earth.

For all they of Muscovy, and all Englishmen maken him gifts, and he keepeth the gifts, and he keepeth his own counsel. For his lond lieth between Ynde and the folk of Muscovy, wherefore both Englishmen and men of Muscovy would fain have him friendly, yea, and independent. Wherefore they of both parties give him clocks, and watches, and stars, and crosses, and culverins, and now and again they let cut the throats of his men some deal, and pill his country. Thereby they both set up their rest that the Emir will be independent, yea, and friendly. But his men love him not, neither love they the English nor the Muscovy folk, for they are worshippers of Mahound, and endure not Christian men. And they love not them that cut their throats, and burn their country.

Now they of Muscovy ben Devyls, und they ben subtle for to make a thing seme otherwise than it is, for to deceive mankind. Wherefore Englishmen putten no trust in them of Muscovy, save only the Englishmen ciept Radicals, for they make as if they loved these Develes, out of the fear and dread of war wherein they go, and would be slaves sooner than fight. But the folk of Ynde know not what shall befall, nor whether they of Muscovy will take the Lond, or Englishmen shall keep it, so that their hearts may not enduren for drede. And methinks that soon shall Englishmen and Muscovy folk put their bodies in adventure, and war one with another, and all for the way to Ynde.

But St. George for Englond, I say, and so enough; and may the Seyntes hele thee, Sir John, of thy Gowtes Artetykes, that thee tormenten. But to thy Boke I list not to give no credence.

XII

To Alexandre Dumas

Sir,—There are moments when the wheels of life, even of such a life as yours, run slow, and when mistrust and doubt overshadow even the most intrepid disposition. In such a moment, towards the ending of your days, you said to your son, M. Alexandre Dumas, 'I seem to see myself set on a pedestal which trembles as if it were founded on the sands.' These sands, your uncounted volumes, are all of gold, and make a foundation more solid than the rock. As well might the singer of Odysseus, or the authors of the 'Arabian Nights', or the first inventors of the stories of Boccaccio, believe that their works were perishable (their names, indeed, have perished), as the creator of 'Les Trois Mousquetaires' alarm himself with the thought that the world could ever forget Alexandre Dumas.

Than yours there has been no greater nor more kindly and beneficent force in modern letters. To Scott, indeed, you owed the first impulse of your genius; but, once set in motion, what miracles could it not accomplish? Our dear Porthos was overcome, at last, by a superhuman burden; but your imaginative strength never found a task too great for it. What an extraordinary vigour, what health, what an overflow of force was yours! It is good, in a day of small and laborious ingenuities, to breathe the free air of your books, and dwell in the company of Dumas's men—so gallant, so frank, so indomitable, such swordsmen, and such trenchermen. Like M. de Rochefort in 'Vingt Ans Aprés,' like that prisoner of the Bastille, your genius 'n'est que d'un parti, c'est du parti du grand air.'

There seems to radiate from you a still persistent energy and enjoyment; in that current of strength not only your characters live, frolic, kindly, and sane, but even your very collaborators were animated by the virtue which went out of you. How else can we explain it, the dreary charge which feeble and envious tongues have brought against you, in England and at home? They say you employed in your novels and dramas that vicarious aid which, in the slang of the studio, the 'sculptor's ghost' is fabled to afford.

Well, let it be so; these ghosts, when uninspired by you, were faint and impotent as 'the strengthless tribes of the dead' in Homer's Hades, before Odysseus had poured forth the blood that gave them a momentary valour. It was from you and your inexhaustible vitality that these collaborating spectres drew what life they possessed; and when they parted from you they shuddered back into their nothingness. Where are the plays, where the romances which Maquet and the rest wrote in their own strength? They are forgotten with last year's snows; they have passed into the wide waste-paper basket of the world. You say of D'Artagnan, when severed from his three friends—from Porthos, Athos, and Aramis— 'he felt that he could do nothing, save on the condition that each of these companions yielded to him, if one may so speak, a share of that electric fluid which was his gift from heaven.'

No man of letters ever had so great a measure of that gift as you; none gave of it more freely to all who came—to the chance associate of the hour, as to the characters, all so burly and full-blooded, who flocked from your brain. Thus it was that you failed when you approached the supernatural. Your ghosts had too much flesh and blood, more than the living persons of feebler fancies. A writer so fertile, so rapid, so masterly in the ease with which he worked, could not escape the reproaches of barren envy. Because you overflowed with wit, you could not be 'serious;' Because you created with a word, you were said to scamp your work; because you were never dull, never pedantic, incapable of greed, you were to be censured as desultory, inaccurate, and prodigal.

A generation suffering from mental and physical anaemia—a generation devoted to the 'chiselled phrase,' to accumulated 'documents,' to microscopic porings over human baseness, to minute and disgustful records of what in humanity is least human—may readily bring these unregarded and railing accusations. Like one of the great and good-humoured Giants of Rabelais, you may hear the murmurs from afar, and smile with disdain. To you, who can amuse the world—to you who offer it the fresh air of the highway, the battle-field, and the sea—the world must always return, escaping gladly from the boudoirs and the bouges, from the surgeries and hospitals, and dead rooms, of M. Daudet and M. Zola and of the wearisome De Goncourt.

With all your frankness, and with that queer morality of the Camp which, if it swallows a camel now and again, never strains at a gnat, how healthy and wholesome, and even pure, are your romances! You never gloat over sin, nor dabble with an ugly curiosity in the corruptions of sense. The passions in your tales are honourable and brave, the motives are clearly human. Honour, Love, Friendship make the threefold cord, the clue your knights and dames follow through how delightful a labyrinth of adventures! Your greatest books, I take the liberty to maintain, are the Cycle of the Valois ('La Reine Margot, 'La Dame de Montsoreau,' 'Les Quarante-cinq'), and the Cycle of Louis Treize and Louis Quatorze ('Les Trois Mousquetaires,' 'Vingt Ans Aprés,' 'Le Vicomte de Bragelonné); and, beside these two trilogies—a lonely monument, like the sphinx hard by the three pyramids—'Monte Cristo.'

In these romances how easy it would have been for you to burn incense to that great goddess, Lubricity, whom our critic says your people worship. You had Branto'me, you had Tallemant, you had Rétif, and a dozen others, to furnish materials for scenes of voluptuousness and of blood that would have outdone even the present naturalistes. From these alcoves of 'Les Dames Galantes,' and from the torture chambers (M. Zola would not have spared us one starting sinew of brave La Mole on the rack) you turned, as Scott would have turned, without a thought of their profitable literary uses. You had other metal to work on: you gave us that superstitious and tragical true love of La Molés, that devotion— how tender and how pure!—of Bussy for the Dame de Montsoreau. You gave us the valour of D'Artagnan, the strength of Porthos, the melancholy nobility of Athos: Honour, Chivalry, and Friendship. I declare your characters are real people to me and old friends. I cannot bear to read the end of 'Bragelonne,' and to part with them for ever. 'Suppose Perthos, Athos, and Aramis should enter with a noiseless swagger, curling their moustaches.' How we would welcome them, forgiving D'Artagnan even his hateful fourberie in the case of Milady. The brilliance of your dialogue has never been approached: there is wit everywhere; repartees glitter and ring like the flash and clink of small-swords. Then what duels are yours! and what inimitable battle-pieces! I know four good fights of one against a multitude, in literature. These are the Death of Gretir the Strong, the Death of Gunnar of Lithend, the Death of Hereward the Wake, the Death of Bussy d'Amboise. We can compare the strokes of the heroic fighting-times with those described in later days; and, upon my word, I do not know that the short sword of Gretir, or the bill of Skarphedin, or the bow of Gunnar was better wielded than the rapier of your Bussy or the sword and shield of Kingsley's Hereward.

They say your fencing is unhistorical; no doubt it is so, and you knew it. La Mole could not have lunged on Coconnas 'after deceiving circle;' for the parry was not invented except by your immortal Chicot, a genius in advance of his time. Even so Hamlet and Laertes would have fought with shields and axes, not with small swords. But what matters this pedantry? In your works we hear the Homeric Muse again, rejoicing in the clash of steel; and even, at times, your very phrases are unconsciously Homeric.

Look at these men of murder, on the Eve of St. Bartholomew, who flee in terror from the Queen's chamber, and 'find the door too narrow for their flight:' the very words were anticipated in a line of the 'Odyssey' concerning the massacre of the Wooers. And the picture of Catherine de Medicis, prowling 'like a wolf among the bodies and the blood,' in a passage of the Louvre—the picture is taken unwittingly from the 'Iliad.' There was in you that reserve of primitive force, that epic grandeur and simplicity of diction. This is the force that animates 'Monte Cristo,' the earlier chapters, the prison, and the escape. In later volumes of that romance, methinks, you stoop your wing. Of your dramas I have little room, and less skill, to speak. 'Antony,' they tell me, was 'the greatest literary event of its time,' was a restoration of the stage. 'While Victor Hugo needs the cast-off clothes of history, the wardrobe and costume, the sepulchre of Charlemagne, the ghost of Barbarossa, the coffins of Lucretia Borgia, Alexandre Dumas requires no more than a room in an inn, where people meet in riding cloaks, to move the soul with the last degree of terror and of pity.'

The reproach of being amusing has somewhat dimmed your fame—for a moment. The shadow of this tyranny will soon be overpast; and when 'La Curée and 'Pot-Bouillé are more forgotten than 'Le Grand Cyrus,' men and women—and, above all, boys—

will laugh and weep over the page of Alexandre Dumas. Like Scott himself, you take us captive in our childhood. I remember a very idle little boy who was busy with the 'Three Musketeers' when he should have been occupied with 'Wilkins's Latin Prose.' 'Twenty years after' (alas and more) he is still constant to that gallant company; and, at this very moment, is breathlessly wondering whether Grimand will steal M. de Beaufort out of the Cardinal's prison.

XIII

To Theocritus

'Sweet, methinks, is the whispering sound of yonder pine-tree,' so, Theocritus, with that sweet word ade[7], didst thou begin and strike the keynote of thy songs. 'Sweet,' and didst thou find aught of sweet, when thou, like thy Daphnis, didst 'go down the stream, when the whirling wave closed over the man the Muses loved, the man not hated of the Nymphs?' Perchance below those waters of death thou didst find, like thine own Hylas, the lovely Nereids waiting thee, Eunice, and Malis, and Nycheia with her April eyes. In the House of Hades, Theocritus, doth there dwell aught that is fair, and can the low light on the fields of asphodel make thee forget thy Sicily? Nay, methinks thou hast not forgotten, and perchance for poets dead there is prepared a place more beautiful than their dreams. It was well for the later minstrels of another day, it was well for Ronsard and Du Bellay to desire a dim Elysium of their own, where the sunlight comes faintly through the shadow of the earth, where the poplars are duskier, and the waters more pale than in the meadows of Anjou.

There, in that restful twilight, far remote from war and plot, from sword and fire, and from religions that sharpened the steel and lit the torch, there these learned singers would fain have wandered with their learned ladies, satiated with life and in love with an unearthly quiet. But to thee, Theocritus, no twilight of the Hollow

---

[7] Transliterated.

72

Land was dear, but the high suns of Sicily and the brown cheeks of the country maidens were happiness enough. For thee, therefore, methinks, surely is reserved an Elysium beneath the summer of a far-off system, with stars not ours and alien seasons. There, as Bion prayed, shall Spring, the thrice desirable, be with thee the whole year through, where there is neither frost, nor is the heat so heavy on men, but all is fruitful, and all sweet things blossom, and evenly meted are darkness and dawn. Space is wide, and there be many worlds, and suns enow, and the Sun-god surely has had a care of his own. Little didst thou need, in thy native land, the isle of the three capes, little didst thou need but sunlight on land and sea. Death can have shown thee naught dearer than the fragrant shadow of the pines, where the dry needles of the fir are strewn, or glades where feathered ferns make 'a couch more soft than Sleep.' The short grass of the cliffs, too, thou didst love, where thou wouldst lie, and watch, with the tunny watcher till the deep blue sea was broken by the burnished sides of the tunny shoal, and afoam with their gambols in the brine. There the Muses met thee, and the Nymphs, and there Apollo, remembering his old thraldom with Admetus, would lead once more a mortal's flocks, and listen and learn, Theocritus, while thou, like thine own Comatas, 'didst sweetly sing.'

There, methinks, I see thee as in thy happy days, 'reclined on deep beds of fragrant lentisk, lowly strewn, and rejoicing in new stript leaves of the vine, while far above thy head waved many a poplar, many an elm-tree, and close at hand the sacred waters sang from the mouth of the cavern of the nymphs.' And when night came, methinks thou wouldst flee from the merry company and the dancing girls, from the fading crowds of roses or white violets, from the cottabos, and the minstrelsy, and the Bibline wine, from these thou wouldst slip away into the summer night. Then the beauty of life and of the summer would keep thee from thy couch, and wandering away from Syracuse by the sandhills and the sea, thou wouldst watch the low cabin, roofed with grass, where the fishing-rods of reed were leaning against the door, while the Mediterranean floated up her waves, and filled the waste with sound. There didst thou see thine ancient fishermen rising ere the dawn from their bed of dry sea-weed, and heardst them stirring, drowsy, among their fishing gear, and heardst them tell their dreams.

Or again thou wouldst wander with dusty feet through the ways that the dust makes silent, while the breath of the kine, as they were driven forth with the morning, came fresh to thee, and the trailing dewy branch of honeysuckle struck sudden on thy cheek. Thou wouldst see the Dawn awake in rose and saffron across the waters, and Etna, grey and pale against the sky, and the setting crescent would dip strangely in the glow, on her way to the sea. Then, methinks, thou wouldst murmur, like thine own Simaetha, the love-lorn witch, 'Farewell, Selene, bright and fair; farewell, ye other stars, that follow the wheels of the quiet Night.' Nay, surely it was in such an hour that thou didst behold the girl as she burned the laurel leaves and the barley grain, and melted the waxen image, and called on Selene to bring her lover home. Even so, even now, in the islands of Greece, the setting Moon may listen to the prayers of maidens. 'Bright golden Moon, that now art near the waters, go thou and salute my lover, he that stole my love, and that kissed me, saying "Never will I leave thee." And lo, he hath left me as men leave a field reaped and gleaned, like a church where none cometh to pray, like a city desolate.'

So the girls still sing in Greece, for though the Temples have fallen, and the wandering shepherds sleep beneath the broken columns of the god's house in Selinus, yet these ancient fires burn still to the old divinities in the shrines of the hearths of the peasants. It is none of the new creeds that cry, in the dirge of the Sicilian shepherds of our time, 'Ah, light of mine eyes, what gift shall I send thee, what offering to the other world? The apple fadeth, the quince decayeth, and one by one they perish, the petals of the rose. I will send thee my tears shed on a napkin, and what though it burneth in the flame, if my tears reach thee at the last.'

Yes, little is altered, Theocritus, on these shores beneath the sun, where thou didst wear a tawny skin stripped from the roughest of he-goats, and about thy breast an old cloak buckled with a plaited belt. Thou wert happier there, in Sicily, methinks, and among vines and shadowy lime-trees of Cos, than in the dust, and heat, and noise of Alexandria. What love of fame, what lust of gold tempted thee away from the red cliffs, and grey olives, and wells of black water wreathed with maidenhair?

> *The music of the rustic flute*
> *Kept not for long its happy country tone;*
> *Lost it too soon, and learned a stormy note*
> *Of men contention tost, of men who groan,*
> *Which tasked thy pipe too sore, and tired thy throat—*
> *It failed, and thou wast mute!*

What hadst thou to make in cities, and what could Ptolemies and Princes give thee better than the goat-milk cheese and the Ptelean wine? Thy Muses were meant to be the delight of peaceful men, not of tyrants and wealthy merchants, to whom they vainly went on a begging errand. 'Who will open his door and gladly receive our Muses within his house, who is there that will not send them back again without a gift? And they with

75

naked feet and looks askance come homewards, and sorely they upbraid me
when they have gone on a vain journey, and listless again in the bottom
of their empty coffer they dwell with heads bowed over their chilly
knees, where is their drear abode, when portionless they return.' How
far happier was the prisoned goat-herd, Comatas, in the fragrant cedar
chest where the blunt-faced bees from the meadow fed him with food of
tender flowers, because still the Muse dropped sweet nectar on his lips!

Thou didst leave the neat-herds and the kine, and the oaks of Himera, the galingale hummed over by the bees, and the pine that dropped her cones, and Amaryllis in her cave, and Bombyca with her feet of carven ivory. Thou soughtest the City, and strife with other singers, and the learned write still on thy quarrels with Apollonius and Callimachus, and Antagoras of Rhodes. So ancient are the hatreds of poets, envy, jealousy, and all unkindness.

Not to the wits of Courts couldst thou teach thy rural song, though all these centuries, more than two thousand years, they have laboured to vie with thee. There has come no new pastoral poet, though Virgil copied thee, and Pope, and Phillips, and all the buckram band of the teacup time; and all the modish swains of France have sung against thee, as the son challenged Athene. They never knew the shepherd's life, the long' winter nights on dried heather by the fire, the long summer days, when over the dry grass all is quiet, and only the insects hum, and the shrunken burn whispers a silver tune. Swains in high-heeled shoon, and lace, shepherdesses in rouge and diamonds, the world is weary of all concerning them, save their images in porcelain, effigies how unlike the golden figures, dedicate to Aphrodite, of Bombyca and Battus. Somewhat, Theocritus, thou hast to answer for, thou that first of men brought the shepherd to Court, and made courtiers wild to go a Maying with the shepherds.

XIV

To Edgar Allan Poe

Sir,—Your English readers, better acquainted with your poems and romances than with your criticisms, have long wondered at the indefatigable hatred which pursues your memory. You, who knew the men, will not marvel that certain microbes of letters, the survivors of your own generation, still harass your name with their malevolence, while old women twitter out their incredible and heeded slanders in the literary papers of New York. But their persistent animosity does not quite suffice to explain the dislike with which many American critics regard the greatest poet, perhaps the greatest literary genius, of their country. With a commendable patriotism, they are not apt to rate native merit too low; and you, I think, are the only example of an American prophet almost without honour in his own country.

The recent publication of a cold, careful, and in many respects admirable study of your career ('Edgar Allan Poe,' by George Woodberry: Houghton, Mifflin and Co., Boston) reminds English readers who have forgotten it, and teaches those who never knew it, that you were, unfortunately, a Reviewer. How unhappy were the necessities, how deplorable the vein, that compelled or seduced a man of your eminence into the dusty and stony ways of contemporary criticism! About the writers of his own generation a leader of that generation should hold his peace, he should neither praise nor blame nor defend his equals; he should not strike one blow at the buzzing ephemerae of letters. The breath of their life is in the columns of 'Literary Gossip;' and they should be allowed to perish with the weekly advertisements on which they pasture. Reviewing, of course, there must needs be; but great minds should only criticise the great who have passed beyond the reach of eulogy or fault-finding.

Unhappily, taste and circumstances combined to make you a censor; you vexed a continent, and you are still unforgiven. What 'irritation of a sensitive nature, chafed by some indefinite sense of wrong,' drove you (in Mr. Longfellow's own words) to attack his pure and beneficent Muse we may never ascertain. But Mr. Longfellow forgave you easily; for pardon comes easily to the great. It was the smaller men, the Daweses, Griswolds, and the like, that knew not how to forget. 'The New Yorkers never forgave him,' says your latest biographer; and one scarcely marvels at the inveteracy of their malice. It was not individual vanity alone, but the whole literary class that you assailed. 'As a literary people,' you wrote, 'we are one vast perambulating humbug.' After that declaration of war you died, and left your reputation to the vanities yet writhing beneath your scorn. They are writhing and writing still. He who knows them need not linger over the attacks and defences of your personal character; he will not waste time on calumnies, tale-bearing, private letters, and all the noisome dust which takes so long in settling above your tomb.

For us it is enough to know that you were compelled to live by your pen, and that in an age when the author of 'To Helen' and' The Cask of Amontillado' was paid at the rate of a dollar a column. When such poverty was the mate of such pride as yours, a misery more deep than that of Burns, an agony longer than Chatterton's, were inevitable and assured. No man was less fortunate than you in the moment of his birth—infelix opportunitate vitae. Had you lived a generation later, honour, wealth, applause, success in Europe and at home, would all have been yours. Within thirty years so great a change has passed over the profession of letters in America; and it is impossible to estimate the rewards which would have fallen to Edgar Poe, had chance made him the contemporary of Mark Twain and of 'Called Back.' It may be that your criticisms helped to bring in the new era, and to lift letters out of the reach of quite unlettered scribblers. Though not a scholar, at least you had a respect for scholarship. You might still marvel over such words as 'objectional' in the new biography of yourself, and might ask what is meant by such a sentence as 'his connection with it had inured to his own benefit by the frequent puffs of himself,' and so forth.

Best known in your own day as a critic, it is as a poet and a writer of short tales that you must live. But to discuss your few and elaborate poems is a waste of time, so completely does your own brief definition of poetry, 'the rhythmic creation of the beautiful,' exhaust your theory, and so perfectly is the theory illustrated by the poems. Natural bent, and reaction against the example of Mr. Longfellow, combined to make you too intolerant of what you call the 'didactic' element in verse. Even if morality be not seven-eighths of our life (the exact proportion as at present estimated), there was a place even on the Hellenic Parnassus for gnomic bards, and theirs in the nature of the case must always be the largest public.

'Music is the perfection of the soul or the idea of poetry,' so you wrote; 'the vagueness of exaltation aroused by a sweet air (which should be indefinite and never too strongly suggestive), is precisely what we should aim at in poetry.' You aimed at that mark, and struck it again and again, notably in 'Helen, thy beauty is to me,' in 'The Haunted Palace,' 'The Valley of Unrest,' and 'The City in the Sea.' But by some Nemesis which might, perhaps, have been foreseen, you are, to the world, the poet of one poem—'The Raven:' a piece in which the music is highly artificial, and the 'exaltation' (what there is of it) by no means particularly 'vague.' So a portion of the public know little of Shelley but the 'Skylark,' and those two incongruous birds, the lark and the raven, bear each of them a poet's name vivu' per ora virum. Your theory of poetry, if accepted, would make you (after the author of 'Kubla Khan') the foremost of the poets of the world; at no long distance would come Mr. William Morris as he was when he wrote 'Golden Wings,' 'The Blue Closet,' and 'The Sailing of the Sword;' and, close up, Mr. Lear, the author of 'The Yongi Bongi Bo,' and the lay of the 'Jumblies.'

On the other hand Homer would sink into the limbo to which you consigned Moliére. If we may judge a theory by its results, when compared with the deliberate verdict of the world, your aesthetic does not seem to hold water. The 'Odyssey' is not really inferior to 'Ulalume,' as it ought to be if your doctrine of poetry were correct, nor 'Le Festin de Pierré to 'Undine.' Yet you deserve the praise of having been constant, in your poetic practice, to your poetic principles—principles commonly deserted by poets who, like Wordsworth, have published their aesthetic system. Your pieces are few; and Dr. Johnson would have called you, like Fielding, 'a barren rascal.' But how can a writer's verses be numerous if with him, as with you, 'poetry is not a pursuit but a passion... which cannot at will be excited with an eye to the paltry compensations or the more paltry commendations of mankind!' Of you it may be said, more truly than Shelley said it of himself, that 'to ask you for anything human, is like asking at a gin-shop for a leg of mutton.'

Humanity must always be, to the majority of men, the true stuff of poetry; and only a minority will thank you for that rare music which (like the strains of the fiddler in the story) is touched on a single string, and on an instrument fashioned from the spoils of the grave. You chose, or you were destined

To vary from the kindly race of men;

and the consequences, which wasted your life, pursue your reputation. For your stories has been reserved a boundless popularity, and that highest success—the success of a perfectly sympathetic translation. By this time, of course, you have made the acquaintance of your translator, M. Charles Baudelaire, who so strenuously shared your views about Mr. Emerson and the Transcendentalists, and who so energetically resisted all those ideas of 'progress' which 'came from Hell or Boston.' On this point, however, the world continues to differ from you and M. Baudelaire, and perhaps there is only the choice between our optimism and universal suicide or universal opium-eating. But to discuss your ultimate ideas is perhaps a profitless digression from the topic of your prose romances.

An English critic (probably a Northerner at heart) has described them as 'Hawthorne and delirium tremens.' I am not aware that extreme orderliness, masterly elaboration, and unchecked progress towards a predetermined effect are characteristics of the visions of delirium. If they be, then there is a deal of truth in the criticism, and a good deal of delirium tremens in your style. But your ingenuity, your completeness, your occasional luxuriance of fancy and wealth of jewel-like words, are not, perhaps, gifts which Mr. Hawthorne had at his command. He was a great writer—the greatest writer in prose fiction whom America has produced. But you and he have not much in common, except a certain mortuary turn of mind and a taste for gloomy allegories about the workings of conscience.

I forbear to anticipate your verdict about the latest essays of

American fiction. These by no means follow in the lines which you laid down about brevity and the steady working to one single effect. Probably you would not be very tolerant (tolerance was not your leading virtue) of Mr. Roe, now your countrymen's favourite novelist. He is long, he is didactic, he is eminently uninspired. In the works of one who is, what you were called yourself, a Bostonian, you would admire, at least, the acute observation, the subtlety, and the unfailing distinction. But, destitute of humour as you unhappily but undeniably were, you would miss, I fear, the charm of 'Daisy Miller.' You would admit the unity of effect secured in 'Washington Square,' though that effect is as remote as possible from the terror of 'The House of Usher' or the vindictive triumph of 'The Cask of Amontillado.'

Farewell, farewell, thou sombre and solitary spirit: a genius tethered to the hack-work of the press, a gentleman among canaille, a poet among poetasters, dowered with a scholar's taste without a scholar's training, embittered by his sensitive scorn, and all unsupported by his consolations.

XV

To Sir Walter Scott, Bart

Rodono, St. Mary's Loch:
Sept. 5, 1885.

Sir,—In your biography it is recorded that you not only won the favour of all men and women; but that a domestic fowl conceived an affection for you, and that a pig, by his will, had never been severed from your company. If some Circe had repeated in my case her favourite miracle of turning mortals into swine, and had given me a choice, into that fortunate pig, blessed among his race, would I have been converted! You, almost alone among men of letters, still, like a living friend, win and charm us out of the past; and if one might call up a poet, as the scholiast tried to call Homer, from the shades, who would not, out of all the rest, demand some hours of your society? Who that ever meddled with letters, what child of the irritable race, possessed even a tithe of your simple manliness, of the heart that never knew a touch of jealousy, that envied no man his laurels, that took honour and wealth as they came, but never would have deplored them had you missed both and remained but the Border sportsman and the Border antiquary?

Were the word 'genial' not so much profaned, were it not misused in easy good-nature, to extenuate lettered and sensual indolence, that worn old term might be applied, above all men, to 'the Shirra.' But perhaps we scarcely need a word (it would be seldom in use) for a character so rare, or rather so lonely, in its nobility and charm as that of Walter Scott. Here, in the heart of your own country, among your own grey round-shouldered hills (each so like the other that the shadow of one falling on its neighbour exactly outlines that neighbour's shape), it is of you and of your works that a native of the Forest is most frequently brought in mind. All the spirits of the river and the hill, all the dying refrains of ballad and the fading echoes of story, all the memory of the wild past, each legend of burn and loch, seem to have combined to inform your spirit, and to secure themselves an immortal life in your song. It is through you that we remember them; and in recalling them, as in treading each hillside in this land, we again remember you and bless you.

It is not 'Sixty Years Since' the echo of Tweed among his pebbles fell for the last time on your ear; not sixty years since, and how much is altered! But two generations have passed; the lad who used to ride from Edinburgh to Abbotsford, carrying new books for you, and old, is still vending, in George Street, old books and new. Of politics I have not the heart to speak. Little joy would you have had in most that has befallen since the Reform Bill was passed, to the chivalrous cry of 'burke Sir Walter.' We are still very Radical in the Forest, and you were taken away from many evils to come. How would the cheek of Walter Scott, or of Leyden, have blushed at the names of Majuba, The Soudan, Maiwand, and many others that recall political cowardice or military incapacity! On the other hand, who but you could have sung the dirge of Gordon, or wedded with immortal verse the names of Hamilton (who fell with Cavagnari), of the two Stewarts, of many another clansman, brave among the bravest! Only he who told how

The stubborn spearmen still made good
Their dark impenetrable wood

84

could have fitly rhymed a score of feats of arms in which, as at M'Neill's Zareeba and at Abu Klea,

> Groom fought like noble, squire like knight,
> As fearlessly and well.

Ah, Sir, the hearts of the rulers may wax faint, and the voting classes may forget that they are Britons; but when it comes to blows our fighting men might cry, with Leyden,

> My name is little Jock Elliot,
> And wha daur meddle wi' me!

Much is changed, in the country-side as well as in the country; but much remains. The little towns of your time are populous and excessively black with the smoke of factories—not, I fear, at present very flourishing. In Galashiels you still see the little change-house and the cluster of cottages round the Laird's lodge, like the clachan of Tully Veolan. But these plain remnants of the old Scotch towns are almost buried in a multitude of 'smoky dwarf houses'—a living poet, Mr. Matthew Arnold, has found the fitting phrase for these dwellings, once for all. All over the Forest the waters are dirty and poisoned: I think they are filthiest below Hawick; but this may be mere local prejudice in a Selkirk man. To keep them clean costs money; and, though improvements are often promised, I cannot see much change for the better. Abbotsford, luckily, is above Galashiels, and only receives the dirt and dyes of Selkirk, Peebles, Walkerburn, and Innerlethen. On the other hand, your ill-omened later dwelling, 'the unhappy palace of your race,' is overlooked by villas that prick a cockney ear among their larches, hotels of the future. Ah, Sir, Scotland is a strange place. Whisky is exiled from some of our caravanserais, and they have banished Sir John Barleycorn. It seems as if the views of the excellent critic (who wrote your life lately, and said you had left no descendants, le pauvre homme) were beginning to prevail. This pious biographer was greatly shocked by that capital story about the keg of whisky that arrived at the Liddesdale farmer's during family prayers. Your Toryism also was an offence to him.

Among these vicissitudes of things and the overthrow of customs, let us be thankful that, beyond the reach of the manufacturers, the Border country remains as kind and homely as ever. I looked at Ashiestiel some days ago: the house seemed just as it may have been when you left it for Abbotsford, only there was a lawn-tennis net on the lawn, the hill on the opposite bank of the Tweed was covered to the crest with turnips, and the burn did not sing below the little bridge, for in this arid summer the burn was dry. But there was still a grilse that rose to a big March brown in the shrunken stream below Elibank. This may not interest you, who styled yourself

> *No fisher,*
> *But a well-wisher*
> *To the game!*

Still, as when you were thinking over Marmion, a man might have 'grand gallops among the hills'—those grave wastes of heather and bent that sever all the watercourses and roll their sheep-covered pastures from Dollar Law to White Combe, and from White Combe to the Three Brethren Cairn and the Windburg and Skelf-hill Pen. Yes, Teviotdale is pleasant still, and there is not a drop of dye in the water, purior electro, of Yarrow. St. Mary's Loch lies beneath me, smitten with wind and rain—the St. Mary's of North and of the Shepherd. Only the trout, that see a myriad of artificial flies, are shyer than of yore. The Shepherd could no longer fill a cart up

Meggat with trout so much of a size that the country people took them for herrings.

The grave of Piers Cockburn is still not desecrated: hard by it lies, within a little wood; and beneath that slab of old sandstone, and the graven letters, and the sword and shield, sleep 'Piers Cockburn and Marjory his wife.' Not a hundred yards off was the castle door where they hanged him; this is the tomb of the ballad, and the lady that buried him rests now with her wild lord.

> Oh, wat ye no my heart was sair,
> When I happit the mouls on his yellow hair;
> Oh, wat ye no my heart was wae,
> When I turned about and went my way![8]

Here too hearts have broken, and there is a sacredness in the shadow and beneath these clustering berries of the rowan-trees. That sacredness, that reverent memory of our old land, it is always and inextricably blended with our memories, with our thoughts, with our love of you. Scotchmen, methinks, who owe so much to you, owe you most for the example you gave of the beauty of a life of honour, showing them what, by Heaven's blessing, a Scotchman still might be.

May 16. William Cokburne of Henderland, convicted (in presence of the King) of high treason committed by him in bringing Alexander Forestare and his son, Englishmen, to the plundering of

---

[8] Lord Napier and Ettrick points out to me that, unluckily, the tradition is erroneous. Piers was not executed at all. William Cockburn suffered in Edinburgh. But the Border Minstrelsy overrides history.
Criminal Trials in Scotland by Robert Pitcairn, Esq. Vol. i. part I. p. 144, A. D. 1530. 17 Jac. V.

Archibald Somervile; and for treasunably bringing certain Englishmen to the lands of Glenquhome; and for common theft, common reset of theft, out-putting and in-putting thereof. Sentence. For which causes and crimes he has forfeited his life, lands, and goods, movable and immovable; which shall be escheated to the King. Beheaded.

Words, empty and unavailing—for what words of ours can speak our thoughts or interpret our affections! From you first, as we followed the deer with King James, or rode with William of Deloraine on his midnight errand, did we learn what Poetry means and all the happiness that is in the gift of song. This and more than may be told you gave us, that are not forgetful, not ungrateful, though our praise be unequal to our gratitude. Fungor inani munere!

XVI

To Eusebius of Caesarea

(Concerning the Gods of the Heathen)

Touching the Gods of the Heathen, most reverend Father, thou art
not ignorant that even now, as in the time of thy probation on earth,
there is great dissension. That these feigned Deities and idols, the
work of men's hands, are no longer worshipped thou knowest;
neither do men eat meat offered to idols. Even as spoke that last
Oracle which murmured forth, the latest and the only true voice
from Delphi, even so 'the fair-wrought court divine hath fallen; no
more hath Phoebus his home, no more his laurel-bough, nor the
singing well of water; nay, the sweet-voiced water is silent.' The
fane is ruinous, and the images of men's idolatry are dust.

Nevertheless, most worshipful, men do still dispute about the
beginnings of those sinful Gods: such as Zeus, Athene, and
Dionysus: and marvel how first they won their dominion over the
souls of the foolish peoples. Now, concerning these things there is
not one belief, but many; howbeit, there are two main kinds of
opinion. One sect of philosophers believes—as thyself, with
heavenly learning, didst not vainly persuade—that the Gods were
the inventions of wild and bestial folk, who, long before cities were
builded or life was honourably ordained, fashioned forth evil spirits
in their own savage likeness; ay, or in the likeness of the very beasts
that perish. To this judgment, as it is set forth in thy Book of the
Preparation for the Gospel, I, humble as I am, do give my consent.

But on the other side are many and learned men, chiefly of the tribes of the Alemanni, who have almost conquered the whole inhabited world. These, being unwilling to suppose that the Hellenes were in bondage to superstitions handed down from times of utter darkness and a bestial life, do chiefly hold with the heathen philosophers, even with the writers whom thou, most venerable, didst confound with thy wisdom and chasten with the scourge of small cords of thy wit.

Thus, like the heathen, our doctors and teachers maintain that the Gods of the nations were, in the beginning, such pure natural creatures as the blue sky, the sun, the air, the bright dawn, and the fire; but, as time went on, men, forgetting the meaning of their own speech and no longer understanding the tongue of their own fathers, were misled and beguiled into fashioning all those lamentable tales: as that Zeus, for love of mortal women, took the shape of a bull, a ram, a serpent, an ant, an eagle, and sinned in such wise as it is a shame even to speak of.

Behold, then, most worshipful, how these doctors and learned men argue, even like the philosophers of the heathen whom thou didst confound. For they declare the Gods to have been natural elements, sun and sky and storm, even as did thy opponents; and, like them, as thou saidst, 'they are nowise at one with each other in their explanations.' For of old some boasted that Hera was the Air; and some that she signified the love of woman and man; and some that she was the waters above the Earth; and others that she was the Earth beneath the waters; and yet others that she was the Night, for that Night is the shadow of Earth: as if, forsooth, the men who first worshipped Hera had understanding of these things! And when Hera and Zeus quarrel unseemly (as Homer declareth), this meant (said the learned in thy days) no more than the strife and confusion of the elements, and was not in the beginning an idle slanderous tale.

To all which, most worshipful, thou didst answer wisely: saying that Hera could not be both night, and earth, and water, and air, and the love of sexes, and the confusion of the elements; but that all these opinions were vain dreams, and the guesses of the learned. And why—thou saidst—even if the Gods were pure natural creatures, are such foul things told of them in the Mysteries as it is not fitting for me to declare. 'These wanderings, and drinkings, and loves, and corruptions, that would be shameful in men, why,' thou saidst, 'were they attributed to the natural elements; and wherefore did the Gods constantly show themselves, like the sorcerers called were-wolves, in the shape of the perishable beasts?' But, mainly, thou didst argue that, till the philosophers of the heathen were agreed among themselves, not all contradicting each the other, they had no semblance of a sure foundation for their doctrine.

To all this and more, most worshipful Father, I know not what the heathen answered thee. But, in our time, the learned men who stand to it that the heathen Gods were in the beginning the pure elements, and that the nations, forgetting their first love and the significance of their own speech, became confused and were betrayed into foul stories about the pure Gods—these learned men, I say, agree no whit among themselves. Nay, they differ one from another, not less than did Plutarch and Porphyry and Theagenes, and the rest whom thou didst laugh to scorn. Bear with me, Father, while I tell thee how the new Plutarchs and Porphyrys do contend among themselves; and yet these differences of theirs they call 'Science'!

Consider the goddess Athene, who sprang armed from the head of

91

Zeus, even as—among the fables of the poor heathen folk of seas thou never knewest—goddesses are fabled to leap out from the armpits or feet of their fathers. Thou must know that what Plato, in the 'Cratylus,' made Socrates say in jest, the learned among us practise in sad earnest. For, when they wish to explain the nature of any God, they first examine his name, and torment the letters thereof, arranging and altering them according to their will, and flying off to the speech of the Indians and Medes and Chaldeans, and other Barbarians, if Greek will not serve their turn. How saith Socrates? 'I bethink me of a very new and ingenious idea that occurs to me; and, if I do not mind, I shall be wiser than I should be by to-morrow's dawn. My notion is that we may put in and pull out letters at pleasure and alter the accents.' Even so do our learned— not at pleasure, maybe, but according to certain fixed laws (so they declare); yet none the more do they agree among themselves. And I deny not that they discover many things true and good to be known; but, as touching the names of the Gods, their learning, as it standeth, is confusion. Look, then, at the goddess Athene: taking one example out of hundreds. We have dwelling in our coasts Muellerus, the most erudite of the doctors of the Alemanni, and the most golden-mouthed. Concerning Athene, he saith that her name is none other than, in the ancient tongue of the Brachmanae, Ahana', which, being interpreted, means the Dawn. 'And that the morning light,' saith he, 'offers the best starting-point; for the later growth of Athene has been proved, I believe, beyond the reach of doubt or even cavil.[9]

Yet this same doctor candidly lets us know that another of his nation, the witty Benfeius, hath devised another sense and origin of Athene, taken from the speech of the old Medes. But Muellerus

---

[9] 'The Lesson of Jupiter.'—Nineteenth Century, October, 1885.

declares to us that whosoever shall examine the contention of Benfeius 'will be bound, in common honesty, to confess that it is untenable.' This, Father, is one for Benfeius, as the saying goes. And as Muellerus holds that these matters 'admit of almost mathematical precision,' it would seem that Benfeius is but a Dummkopf, as the Alemanni say, in their own language, when they would be pleasant among themselves.

Now, wouldst thou credit it? despite the mathematical plainness of the facts, other Alemanni agree neither with Muellerus, nor yet with Benfeius, and will neither hear that Athene was the Dawn, nor yet that she is 'the feminine of the Zend Thra'eta'na athwya'na.' Lo, you! how Prellerus goes about to show that her name is drawn not from Ahana' and the old Brachmanae, nor athwya'na and the old Medes, but from 'the root aith[10], whence aither*, the air, or ath*, whence anthos*, a flower.' Yea, and Prellerus will have it that no man knows the verity of this matter. None the less he is very bold, and will none of the Dawn; but holds to it that Athene was, from the first, 'the clear pure height of the Air, which is exceeding pure in Attica.'

Now, Father, as if all this were not enough, comes one Roscherus in, with a mighty great volume on the Gods, and Furtwaenglerus, among others, for his ally. And these doctors will neither with Rueckertus and Hermannus, take Athene for 'wisdom in person;' nor with Welckerus and Prellerus, for 'the goddess of air;' nor even, with Muellerus and mathematical certainty, for 'the Morning-Red:' but they say that Athene is the 'black thunder-cloud, and the lightning that leapeth therefrom'! I make no doubt that other Alemanni are of other minds: quot Alemanni tot sententiae.

---

[10] Transliterated from Greek.

93

Yea, as thou saidst of the learned heathen, Oude gar allelois symphona physiologousis. Yet these disputes of theirs they call 'Science'! But if any man says to the learned: 'Best of men, you are erudite, and laborious and witty; but, till you are more of the same mind, your opinions cannot be styled knowledge. Nay, they are at present of no avail whereon to found any doctrine concerning the Gods'—that man is railed at for his 'mean' and 'weak' arguments.

Was it thus, Father, that the heathen railed against thee? But I must still believe, with thee, that these evil tales of the Gods were invented 'when man's life was yet brutish and wandering' (as is the life of many tribes that even now tell like tales), and were maintained in honour of the later Greeks 'because none dared alter the ancient beliefs of his ancestors.' Farewell, Father; and all good be with thee, wishes thy well-wisher and thy disciple.

XVII

To Percy Bysshe Shelley

Sir,—In your lifetime on earth you were not more than commonly curious as to what was said by 'the herd of mankind,' if I may quote your own phrase. It was that of one who loved his fellow-men, but did not in his less enthusiastic moments overestimate their virtues and their discretion. Removed so far away from our hubbub, and that world where, as you say, we 'pursue our serious folly as of old,' you are, one may guess, but moderately concerned about the fate of your writings and your reputation. As to the first, you have somewhere said, in one of your letters, that the final judgment on your merits as a poet is in the hands of posterity, and that you fear the verdict will be 'Guilty,' and the sentence 'Death.' Such apprehensions cannot have been fixed or frequent in the mind of one whose genius burned always with a clearer and steadier flame to the last. The jury of which you spoke has met: a mixed jury and a merciful. The verdict is 'Well done,' and the sentence Immortality of Fame. There have been, there are, dissenters; yet probably they will be less and less heard as the years go on.

One judge, or juryman, has made up his mind that prose was your true province, and that your letters will outlive your lays. I know not whether it was the same or an equally well-inspired critic, who spoke of your most perfect lyrics (so Beau Brummell spoke of his ill-tied cravats) as 'a gallery of your failures.' But the general voice does not echo these utterances of a too subtle intellect. At a famous University (not your own) once existed a band of men known as

'The Trinity Sniffers.' Perhaps the spirit of the sniffer may still inspire some of the jurors who from time to time make themselves heard in your case. The 'Quarterly Review', I fear, is still unreconciled. It regards your attempts as tainted by the spirit of 'The Liberal Movement in English Literature;' and it is impossible, alas! to maintain with any success that you were a Throne and Altar Tory. At Oxford you are forgiven; and the old rooms where you let the oysters burn (was not your founder, King Alfred, once guilty of similar negligence?) are now shown to pious pilgrims.

But Conservatives, 't is rumoured, are still averse to your opinions, and are believed to prefer to yours the works of the Reverend Mr. Keble, and, indeed, of the clergy in general. But, in spite of all this, your poems, like the affections of the true lovers in Theocritus, are still 'in the mouths of all, and chiefly on the lips of the young.' It is in your lyrics that you live, and I do not mean that every one could pass an examination in the plot of "Prometheus Unbound" Talking of this piece, by the way, a Cambridge critic finds that it reveals in you a hankering after life in a cave—doubtless an unconsciously inherited memory from cave-man. Speaking of cave-man reminds me that you once spoke of deserting song for prose, and of producing a history of the moral, intellectual, and political elements in human society, which, we now agree, began, as Asia would fain have ended, in a cave.

Fortunately you gave us 'Adonai, and 'Hellas' instead of this treatise, and we have now successfully written the natural history of Man for ourselves. Science tells us that before becoming cave-dweller he was a brute; Experience daily proclaims that he constantly reverts to his original condition. L'homme est un méchant animal, in spite of your boyish efforts to add pretty girls 'to the list of the good, the disinterested, and the free.'

Ah, not in the wastes of Speculation, nor the sterile din of Politics, were 'the haunts meet for thee.' Watching the yellow bees in the ivy bloom, and the reflected pine forest in the water-pools, watching the sunset as it faded, and the dawn as it fired, and weaving all fair and fleeting things into a tissue where light and music were at one, that was the task of Shelley! 'To ask you for anything human,' you said, 'was like asking for a leg of mutton at a gin-shop.' Nay, rather, like asking Apollo and Hebe, in the Olympian abodes, to give us beef for ambrosia, and port for nectar. Each poet gives what he has, and what he can offer; you spread before us fairy bread, and enchanted wine, and shall we turn away, with a sneer, because, out of all the multitudes of singers, one is spiritual and strange, one has seen Artemis unveiled? One, like Anchises, has been beloved of the Goddess, and his eyes, when he looks on the common works of common men, are, like the eyes of Anchises, blind with excess of light. Let Shelley sing of what he saw, what none saw but Shelley!

Notwithstanding the popularity of your poems (the most romantic of things didactic), our world is no better than the world you knew. This will disappoint you, who had 'a passion for reforming it.' Kings and priests are very much where you left them. True, we have a poet who assails them, at large, frequently and fearlessly; yet Mr. Swinburne has never, like 'kind Hunt,' been in prison, nor do we fear for him a charge of treason. Moreover, chemical science has discovered new and ingenious ways of destroying principalities and powers. You would be interested in the methods, but your peaceful Revolutionism, which disdained physical force, would regret their application.

Our foreign affairs are not in a state which even you would consider satisfactory; for we have just had to contend with a Revolt of Islam, and we still find in Russia exactly the qualities which you recognised and described. We have a great statesman whose methods and eloquence somewhat resemble those you attribute to Laon and Prince Athanase. Alas! he is a youth of more than seventy summers; and not in his time will Prometheus retire to a cavern and pass a peaceful millennium in twining buds and beams.

In domestic affairs most of the Reforms you desired to see have been carried. Ireland has received Emancipation, and almost everything else she can ask for. I regret to say that she is still unhappy; her wounds unstanched, her wrongs unforgiven. At home we have enfranchised the paupers, and expect the most happy results. Paupers (as Mr. Gladstone says) are 'our own flesh and blood,' and, as we compel them to be vaccinated, so we should permit them to vote. Is it a dream that Mr. Jesse Collings (how you would have loved that man!) has a Bill for extending the priceless boon of the vote to inmates of Pauper Lunatic Asylums? This may prove that last element in the Elixir of political happiness which we have sought in vain. Atheists, you will regret to hear, are still unpopular; but the new Parliament has done something for Mr. Bradlaugh. You should have known our Charles while you were in the 'Queen Mab' stage. I fear you wandered, later, from his robust condition of intellectual development.

As to your private life, many biographers contrive to make public as much of it as possible. Your name, even in life, was, alas! a kind of ducdame to bring people of no very great sense into your circle. This curious fascination has attracted round your memory a feeble folk of commentators, biographers, anecdotists, and others of the tribe. They swarm round you like carrion-flies round a sensitive plant, like night-birds bewildered by the sun. Men of sense and taste have written on you, indeed; but your weaker admirers are now disputing as to whether it was your heart, or a less dignified and most troublesome organ, which escaped the flames of the funeral pyre. These biographers fight terribly among themselves, and vainly prolong the memory of 'old unhappy far-off things, and sorrows long ago.' Let us leave them and their squabbles over what is unessential, their raking up of old letters and old stories.

The town has lately yawned a weary laugh over an enemy of yours, who has produced two heavy volumes, styled by him 'The Real Shelley.' The real Shelley, it appears, was Shelley as conceived of by a worthy gentleman so prejudiced and so skilled in taking up things by the wrong handle that I wonder he has not made a name in the exact science of Comparative Mythology. He criticises you in the spirit of that Christian Apologist, the Englishman who called you 'a damned Atheist' in the post-office at Pisa. He finds that you had 'a little turned-up nose,' a feature no less important in his system than was the nose of Cleopatra (according to Pascal) in the history of the world. To be in harmony with your nose, you were a 'phenomenal' liar, an ill-bred, ill-born, profligate, partly insane, an evil-tempered monster, a self-righteous person, full of self-approbation—in fact you were the Beast of this pious Apocalypse. Your friend Dr. Lind was an embittered and scurrilous apothecary, 'a bad old man.' But enough of this inopportune brawler. For Humanity, of which you hoped such great things, Science predicts extinction in a night of Frost. The sun will grow cold, slowly—as slowly as doom came on Jupiter in your 'Prometheus,' but as surely. If this nightmare be fulfilled, perhaps the Last Man, in some fetid hut on the ice-bound Equator, will read. by a fading lamp charged with the dregs of the oil in his cruse, the poetry of Shelley. So reading, he, the latest of his race, will not wholly be deprived of those sights which alone (says the nameless Greek) make life worth enduring. In your verse he will have sight of sky, and sea, and cloud, the gold of dawn and the gloom of earthquake and eclipse, he will be face to face, in fancy, with the great powers that are dead, sun, and ocean, and the illimitable azure of the heavens. In Shelley's poetry, while Man endures, all those will survive; for your 'voice is as the voice of winds and tides,' and perhaps more deathless than all of these, and only perishable with the perishing of the human spirit.

XVIII

To Monsieur de Moliére, Valet de Chambre du Roi

Monsieur,—With what awe does a writer venture into the presence of the great Moliére! As a courtier in your time would scratch humbly (with his comb!) at the door of the Grand Monarch, so I presume to draw near your dwelling among the Immortals. You, like the king who, among all his titles, has now none so proud as that of the friend of Moliére—you found your dominions small, humble, and distracted; you raised them to the dignity of an empire: what Louis XIV. did for France you achieved for French comedy; and the ba'ton of Scapin still wields its sway though the sword of Louis was broken at Blenheim. For the King the Pyrenees, or so he fancied, ceased to exist; by a more magnificent conquest you overcame the Channel. If England vanquished your country's arms, it was through you that France ferum victorem cepit, and restored the dynasty of Comedy to the land whence she had been driven. Ever since Dryden borrowed 'L'Etourdi,' our tardy apish nation has lived (in matters theatrical) on the spoils of the wits of France.

In one respect, to be sure, times and manners have altered. While you lived, taste kept the French drama pure; and it was the congenial business of English playwrights to foist their rustic grossness and their large Fescennine jests into the urban page of Moliére. Now they are diversely occupied; and it is their affair to lend modesty where they borrow wit, and to spare a blush to the cheek of the Lord Chamberlain. But still, as has ever been our wont since Etherege saw, and envied, and imitated your successes—still we pilfer the plays of France, and take our bien, as you said in your lordly manner, wherever we can find it. We are the privateers of the stage; and it is rarely, to be sure, that a comedy pleases the town which has not first been 'cut out' from the countrymen of Moliére. Why this should be, and what 'tenebriferous star' (as Paracelsus, your companion in the 'Dialogues des Morts,' would have believed) thus darkens the sun of English humour, we know not; but certainly our dependence on France is the sincerest tribute to you. Without you, neither Rotrou, nor Corneille, nor 'a wilderness of monkeys' like Scarron, could ever have given Comedy to France and restored her to Europe.

While we owe to you, Monsieur, the beautiful advent of Comedy, fair and beneficent as Peace in the play of Aristophanes, it is still to you that we must turn when of comedies we desire the best. If you studied with daily and nightly care the works of Plautus and Terence, if you 'let no musty bouquin escape you' (so your enemies declared), it was to some purpose that you laboured. Shakespeare excepted, you eclipsed all who came before you; and from those that follow, however fresh, we turn: we turn from Regnard and Beaumarchais, from Sheridan: and Goldsmith, from Musset and Pailleron and Labiche, to that crowded world of your creations. 'Creations' one may well say, for you anticipated Nature herself: you gave us, before she did, in Alceste a Rousseau who was a gentleman not a lacquey; in a mot of Don Juan's, the secret of the new Religion and the watchword of Comte, l'amour de l'humanité.

Before you where can we find, save in Rabelais, a Frenchman with humour; and where, unless it be in Montaigne, the wise philosophy of a secular civilisalion? With a heart the most tender, delicate, loving, and generous, a heart often in agony and torment, you had to make life endurable (we cannot doubt it) without any whisper of promise, or hope, or warning from Religion. Yes, in an age when the greatest mind of all, the mind of Pascal, proclaimed that the only help was in voluntary blindness, that the only chance was to hazard all on a bet at evens, you, Monsieur, refused to be blinded, or to pretend to see what you found invisible.

In Religion you beheld no promise of help. When the Jesuits and Jansenists of your time saw, each of them, in Tartufe the portrait of their rivals (as each of the laughable Marquises in your play conceived that you were girding at his neighbour), you all the while were mocking every credulous excess of Faith. In the sermons preached to Agnés we surely hear your private laughter; in the arguments for credulity which are presented to Don Juan by his valet we listen to the eternal self-defence of superstition. Thus, desolate of belief, you sought for the permanent element of life—precisely where Pascal recognised all that was most fleeting and unsubstantial—in divertissement; in the pleasure of looking on, a spectator of the accidents of existence, an observer of the follies of mankind. Like the Gods of the Epicurean, you seem to regard our life as a play that is played, as a comedy; yet how often the tragic note comes in! What pity, and in the laughter what an accent of tears, as of rain in the wind! No comedian has been so kindly and human as you; none has had a heart, like you, to feel for his butts, and to leave them sometimes, in a sense, superior to their tormentors. Sganarelle, M. de Pourceaugnac, George Dandin, and the rest—our sympathy, somehow, is with them, after all; and M. de Pourceaugnac is a gentleman, despite his misadventures.

Though triumphant Youth and malicious Love in your plays may batter and defeat Jealousy and Old Age, yet they have not all the victory, or you did not mean that they should win it. They go off with laughter, and their victim with a grimace; but in him we, that are past our youth, behold an actor in an unending tragedy, the defeat of a generation. Your sympathy is not wholly with the dogs that are having their day; you can throw a bone or a crust to the dog that has had his, and has been taught that it is over and ended. Yourself not unlearned in shame, in jealousy, in endurance of the wanton pride of men (how could the poor player and the husband of Céliméne be untaught in that experience?), you never sided quite heartily, as other comedians have done, with young prosperity and rank and power.

I am not the first who has dared to approach you in the Shades; for just after your own death the author of 'Les Dialogues des Morts' gave you Paracelsus as a companion, and the author of 'Le Jugement de Pluton' made the 'mighty warder' decide that 'Moliére should not talk philosophy.' These writers, like most of us, feel that, after all, the comedies of the Contemplateur, of the translator of Lucretius, are a philosophy of life in themselves, and that in them we read the lessons of human experience writ small and clear.

What comedian but Moliére has combined with such depths—with the indignation of Alceste, the self-deception of Tartufe, the blasphemy of Don Juan—such wildness of irresponsible mirth, such humour, such wit! Even now, when more than two hundred years have sped by, when so much water has flowed under the bridges and has borne away so many trifles of contemporary mirth (cetera fluminis ritu feruntur), even now we never laugh so well as when Mascarille and Vadius and M. Jourdain tread the boards in the Maison de Moliére. Since those mobile dark brows of yours ceased to make men laugh, since your voice denounced the 'demoniac' manner of contemporary tragedians, I take leave to think that no player has been more worthy to wear the canons of Mascarille or the gown of Vadius than M. Coquelin of the Comédie Francaise. In him you have a successor to your Mascarille so perfect, that the ghosts of play-goers of your date might cry, could they see him, that Moliére had come again. But, with all respect to the efforts of the fair, I doubt if Mdlle. Barthet, or Mdme. Croizette herself, would reconcile the town to the loss of the fair De Brie, and Madeleine, and the first, the true Céliméne, Armande. Yet had you ever so merry a soubrette as Mdme. Samary, so exquisite a Nicole?

Denounced, persecuted, and buried hugger-mugger two hundred years ago, you are now not over-praised, but more worshipped, with more servility and ostentation, studied with more prying curiosity than you may approve. Are not the Moliéristes a body who carry adoration to fanaticism? Any scrap of your handwriting (so few are these), any anecdote even remotely touching on your life, any fact that may prove your house was numbered 15 not 22, is eagerly seized and discussed by your too minute historians. Concerning your private life, these men often write more like malicious enemies than friends; repeating the fabulous scandals of Le Boulanger, and trying vainly to support them by grubbing in dusty parish registers. It is most necessary to defend you from your friends—from such friends as the veteran and inveterate M. Arséne Houssaye, or the industrious but puzzle-headed M. Loiseleur. Truly they seek the living among the dead, and the immortal Moliére among the sweepings of attorneys' offices. As I regard them (for I have tarried in their tents) and as I behold their trivialities—the exercises of men who neglect Moliérés works to write about Moliére's great-grandmother's second-best bed—I sometimes wish that Moliére were here to write on his devotees a new comedy, 'Les Moliéristes.' How fortunate were they, Monsieur, who lived and worked with you, who saw you day by day, who were attached, as Lagrange tells us, by the kindest loyalty to the best and most honourable of men, the most open-handed in friendship, in charity the most delicate, of the heartiest sympathy! Ah, that for one day I could behold you, writing in the study, rehearsing on the stage, musing in the lace-seller's shop, strolling through the Palais, turning over the new books at Billaine's, dusting your ruffles among the old volumes on the sunny stalls. Would that, through the ages, we could hear you after supper, merry with Boileau, and with Racine,—not yet a traitor,—laughing over Chapelain, combining to gird at him in an epigram, or mocking at Cotin, or talking your favourite philosophy, mindful of Descartes. Surely of all the wits none was ever so good a man, none ever made life so rich with humour and friendship.

XIX

To Robert Burns

Sir,—Among men of Genius, and especially among Poets, there are some to whom we turn with a peculiar and unfeigned affection; there are others whom we admire rather than love. By some we are won with our will, by others conquered against our desire. It has been your peculiar fortune to capture the hearts of a whole people—a people not usually prone to praise, but devoted with a personal and patriotic loyalty to you and to your reputation. In you every Scot who is a Scot sees, admires, and compliments Himself, his ideal self—independent, fond of whisky, fonder of the lassies; you are the true representative of him and of his nation. Next year will be the hundredth since the press of Kilmarnock brought to light its solitary masterpiece, your Poems; and next year, therefore, methinks, the revenue will receive a welcome accession from the abundance of whisky drunk in your honour. It is a cruel thing for any of your countrymen to feel that, where all the rest love, he can only admire; where all the rest are idolators, he may not bend the knee; but stands apart and beats upon his breast, observing, not adoring—a critic. Yet to some of us—petty souls, perhaps, and envious—that loud indiscriminating praise of 'Robbie Burns' (for so they style you in their Change-house familiarity) has long been ungrateful; and, among the treasures of your songs, we venture to select and even to reject. So it must be! We cannot all love Haggis, nor 'painch, tripe, and thairm,' and all those rural dainties which you celebrate as 'warm-reekin, rich!' 'Rather too rich,' as the Young Lady said on an occasion recorded by Sam Weller.

Auld Scotland wants nae skinking ware
  That jaups in luggies;
But, if ye wish her gratefu' prayer,
  Gie her a Haggis!

*You have given her a Haggis, with a vengeance, and her 'gratefu' prayer'
is*

*yours for ever. But if even an eternity of partridge may pall on the
epicure, so of Haggis too, as of all earthly delights, cometh satiety at
last. And yet what a glorious Haggis it is — the more emphatically rustic
and even Fescennine part of your verse! We have had many a rural bard
since Theocritus 'watched the visionary flocks,' but you are the only
one of them all who has spoken the sincere Doric. Yours is the talk of
the byre and the plough-tail; yours is that large utterance of the early
hinds. Even Theocritus minces matters, save where Lacon and Comatas
quite outdo the swains of Ayrshire. 'But thee, Theocritus, wha matches?'
you ask, and yourself out-match him in this wide rude region, trodden
only by the rural Muse.*

'Thy rural loves are nature's sel';' and the wooer of Jean Armour
speaks more like a true shepherd than the elegant Daphnis of the
'Oaristys.'

Indeed it is with this that moral critics of your life reproach you,
forgetting, perhaps, that in your amours you were but as other
Scotch ploughmen and shepherds of the past and present. Ettrick
may still, with Afghanistan, offer matter for idylls, as Mr. Carlyle
(your antithesis, and the complement of the Scotch character)
supposed; but the morals of Ettrick are those of rural Sicily in old
days, or of Mossgiel in your days. Over these matters the Kirk, with
all her power, and the Free Kirk too, have had absolutely no
influence whatever. To leave so delicate a topic, you were but as

108

other swains, or, as 'that Birkie ca'd a lord,' Lord Byron; only you combined (in certain of your letters) a libertine theory with your practice; you poured out in song your audacious raptures, your half-hearted repentance, your shame and your scorn. You spoke the truth about rural lives and loves. We may like it or dislike it; but we cannot deny the verity.

Was it not as unhappy a thing, Sir, for you, as it was fortunate for Letters and for Scotland, that you were born at the meeting of two ages and of two worlds—precisely in the moment when bookish literature was beginning to reach the people, and when Society was first learning to admit the low-born to her Minor Mysteries? Before you how many singers not less truly poets than yourself—though less versatile not less passionate, though less sensuous not less simple—had been born and had died in poor men's cottages! There abides not even the shadow of a name of the old Scotch song-smiths, of the old ballad-makers. The authors of 'Clerk Saunders,' of 'The Wife of Usher's Well,' of 'Fair Annie,' and 'Sir Patrick Spens,' and 'The Bonny Hind,' are as unknown to us as Homer, whom in their directness and force they resemble. They never, perhaps, gave their poems to writing; certainly they never gave them to the press. On the lips and in the hearts of the people they have their lives; and the singers, after a life obscure and untroubled by society or by fame, are forgotten. 'The Iniquity of Oblivion blindly scattereth his Poppy.'

Had you been born some years earlier you would have been even as these unnamed Immortals, leaving great verses to a little clan—verses retained only by Memory. You would have been but the minstrel of your native valley: the wider world would not have known you, nor you the world. Great thoughts of independence and revolt would never have burned in you; indignation would not have vexed you. Society would not have given and denied her caresses. You would have been happy. Your songs would have lingered in all 'the circle of the summer hills;' and your scorn, your satire, your narrative verse, would have been unwritten or unknown. To the world what a loss! and what a gain to you! We should have possessed but a few of your lyrics, as

> *When o'er the hill the eastern star*
> *Tells bughtin-time is near, my jo;*
> *And owsen frae the furrowed field,*
> *Return sae dowf and wearie O!*

How noble that is, how natural, how unconsciously Greek! You found, oddly, in good Mrs. Barbauld, the merits of the Tenth Muse:

> *In thy sweet sang, Barbauld, survives*
> *Even Sappho's flame!*

But how unconsciously you remind us both of Sappho and of Homer in these strains about the Evening Star and the hour when the Day metenisseto boulytoide?[11] Had you lived and died the pastoral poet of some silent glen, such lyrics could not but have survived; free, too, of all that in your songs reminds us of the Poet's Corner in the 'Kirkcudbright Advertiser.' We should not have read how

> *Phoebus, gilding the brow o' morning,*
> *Banishes ilk darksome shade!*

Still we might keep a love-poem unexcelled by Catullus,

> *Had we never loved sae kindly,*
> *Had we never loved sae blindly,*

---

[11] Transliterated from Greek.

110

> *Never met—or never parted,*
> *We had ne'er been broken-hearted.*

But the letters to Clarinda would have been unwritten, and the thrush would have been untaught in 'the style of the Bird of Paradise.'

A quiet life of song, fallentis semita vitae', was not to be yours. Fate otherwise decreed it. The touch of a lettered society, the strife with the Kirk, discontent with the State, poverty and pride, neglect and success, were needed to make your Genius what it was, and to endow the world with 'Tam o' Shanter,' the 'Jolly Beggars,' and 'Holy Willie's Prayer.' Who can praise them too highly—who admire in them too much the humour, the scorn, the wisdom, the unsurpassed energy and courage? So powerful, so commanding, is the movement of that Beggars' Chorus, that, methinks, it unconsciously echoed in the brain of our greatest living poet when he conceived the Vision of Sin. You shall judge for yourself. Recall:

> *Here's to budgets, bags, and wallets!*
> *Here's to all the wandering train!*
> *Here's our ragged bairns and callers!*
> *One and all cry out, Amen!*
>
> *A fig for those by law protected!*
> *Liberty's a glorious feast!*
> *Courts for cowards were erected!*
> *Churches built to please the priest!*
>
> *Then read this: Drink to lofty hopes that cool*
> *Visions of a perfect state:*
> *Drink we, last, the public fool,*

> *Frantic love and frantic hate.*
> .... *Drink to Fortune, drink to Chance,*
> *While we keep a little breath!*
> *Drink to heavy Ignorance*
> *Hob and nob with brother Death!*

> *Is not the movement the same, though the modern speaks a wilder reclessness?*

So in the best company we leave you, who were the life and soul of so much company, good and bad. No poet, since the Psalmist of Israel, ever gave the world more assurance of a man; none lived a life more strenuous, engaged in an eternal conflict of the passions, and by them overcome—'mighty and mightily fallen.' When we think of you, Byron seems, as Plato would have said, remote by one degree from actual truth, and Musset by a degree more remote than Byron.

XX

To Lord Byron

My Lord, (Do you remember how Leigh Hunt
Enraged you once by writing My dear Byron?)
Books have their fates,—as mortals have who punt,
And yours have entered on an age of iron.
Critics there be who think your satin blunt,
Your pathos, fudge; such perils must environ
Poets who in their time were quite the rage,
Though now there's not a soul to turn their page.

Yes, there is much dispute about your worth,
And much is said which you might like to know
By modern poets here upon the earth,
Where poets live, and love each other so;
And, in Elysium, it may move your mirth
To hear of bards that pitch your praises low,
Though there be some that for your credit stickle,
As—Glorious Mat,—and not inglorious Nichol.

This kind of writing is my pet aversion,
I hate the slang, I hate the personalities,
I loathe the aimless, reckless, loose dispersion,
Of every rhyme that in the singer's wallet is,
I hate it as you hated the Excursion,
But, while no man a hero to his valet is,

113

The hero's still the model; I indite
The kind of rhymes that Byron oft would write.

There's a Swiss critic whom I cannot rhyme to,
  One Scherer, dry as sawdust, grim and prim.
Of him there's much to say, if I had time to
  Concern myself in any wise with him.
He seems to hate the heights he cannot climb to,
He thinks your poetry a coxcomb's whim,
A good deal of his sawdust he has spilt on
Shakspeare, and Moliére, and you, and Milton.

Ay, much his temper is like Vivien's mood,
  Which found not Galahad pure, nor Lancelot brave;
Cold as a hailstorm on an April wood,
  He buries poets in an icy grave,
His Essays—he of the Genevan hood!
  Nothing so good, but better doth he crave.
So stupid and so solemn in his spite
He dares to print that Moliére could not write!

Enough of these excursions; I was saying
  That half our English Bards are turned Reviewers,
And Arnold was discussing and assaying
  The weight and value of that work of yours,
Examining and testing it and weighing,
  And proved, the gems are pure, the gold endures.
While Swinburne cries with an exceeding joy,
the stones are paste, and half the gold, alloy.

In Byron, Arnold finds the greatest force,

Poetic, in this later age of ours
His song, a torrent from a mountain source,
 Clear as the crystal, singing with the showers,
Sweeps to the sea in unrestricted course
 Through banks o'erhung with rocks and sweet with flowers;
None of your brooks that modestly meander,
But swift as Awe along the Pass of Brander.

And when our century has clomb its crest,
 And backward gazes o'er the plains of Time,
And counts its harvest, yours is still the best,
 The richest garner in the field of rhyme
(The metaphoric mixture, 't is confest,
 Is all my own, and is not quite sublime).
But fame's not yours alone; you must divide all
The plums and pudding with the Bard of Rydal!

WORDSWORTH and BYRON, these the lordly names
 And these the gods to whom most incense burns.
'Absurd!' cries Swinburne, and in anger flames,
 And in an AEschylean fury spurns
With impious foot your altar, and exclaims
 And wreathes his laurels on the golden urns
Where Coleridge's and Shelley's ashes lie,
Deaf to the din and heedless of the cry.

For Byron (Swinburne shouts) has never woven
 One honest thread of life within his song;
As Offenbach is to divine Beethoven
 So Byron is to Shelley (This is strong!),
And on Parnassus' peak, divinely cloven,

He may not stand, or stands by cruel wrong;
For Byron's rank (the Examiner has reckoned)
Is in the third class or a feeble second.

'A Bernesque poet' at the very most,
 And never earnest save in politics —
The Pegasus that he was wont to boast
 A blundering, floundering hackney, full of tricks,
A beast that must be driven to the post
 By whips and spurs and oaths and kicks and sticks,
A gasping, ranting, broken-winded brute,
That any judge of Pegasi would shoot;

In sooth, a half-bred Pegasus, and far gone
 In spavin, curb, and half a hundred woes.
And Byron's style is 'jolter-headed jargon;'
 His verse is 'only bearable in prose.'
So living poets write of those that are gone,
 And o'er the Eagle thus the Bantam crows;
And Swinburne ends where Verisopht began,
By owning you 'a very clever man.'

Or rather does not end: he still must utter
 A quantity of the unkindest things.
Ah! were you here, I marvel, would you flutter
 O'er such a foe the tempest of your wings?
'T is 'rant and cant and glare and splash and splutter'
 That rend the modest air when Byron sings.
There Swinburne stops: a critic rather fiery.
Animis caelestibus tantaene irae?

But whether he or Arnold in the right is,
 Long is the argument, the quarrel long;
Non nobis est to settle tantas lites;
 No poet I, to judge of right or wrong:
But of all things I always think a fight is
 The most unpleasant in the lists of song;
When Marsyas of old was flayed, Apollo
Set an example which we need not follow.

The fashion changes! Maidens do not wear,
 As once they wore, in necklaces and lockets
A curl ambrosial of Lord Byron's hair;
 'Don Juan' is not always in our pockets
Nay, a NEW WRITER's readers do not care
 Much for your verse, but are inclined to mock its
Manners and morals. Ay, and most young ladies
To yours prefer the 'Epic' called 'of Hades'!

I do not blame them; I'm inclined to think
 That with the reigning taste 't is vain to quarrel,
And Burns might teach his votaries to drink,
 And Byron never meant to make them moral.
You yet have lovers true, who will not shrink
 From lauding you and giving you the laurel;
The Germans too, those men of blood and iron,
Of all our poets chiefly swear by Byron.

Farewell, thou Titan fairer than the gods!
 Farewell, farewell, thou swift and lovely spirit,
Thou splendid warrior with the world at odds,
 Unpraised, unpraisable, beyond thy merit;

Chased, like Oresres, by the furies' rods,
Like him at length thy peace dost thou inherit;
Beholding whom, men think how fairer far
Than all the steadfast stars the wandering star!

Note Mr. Swlnburne's and Mr. Arnold's diverse views of Byron will be found in the Selections by Mr. Arnold and in the Nineteenth Century.

XXI

To Omar Kha'yya'm

Wise Omar, do the Southern Breezes fling
Above your Grave, at ending of the Spring,
  The Snowdrift of the petals of the Rose,
The wild white Roses you were wont to sing?

Far in the South I know a Land divine,[12]
And there is many a Saint and many a Shrine,
  And over all the shrines the Blossom blows
Of Roses that were dear to you as wine.

You were a Saint of unbelieving days,
Liking your Life and happy in men's Praise;
  Enough for you the Shade beneath the Bough,
Enough to watch the wild World go its Ways.

Dreadless and hopeless thou of Heaven or Hell,
Careless of Words thou hadst not Skill to spell,
  Content to know not all thou knowest now,
What's Death? Doth any Pitcher dread the Well?
The Pitchers we, whose Maker makes them ill,

---

[12] The hills above San Remo, where rose-bushes are planted   by the
shrines. Omar desired that his grave might be where the wind would
scatter rose-leaves over it.

Shall He torment them if they chance to spill?
 Nay, like the broken potsherds are we cast
Forth and forgotten,—and what will be will!

So still were we, before the Months began
That rounded us and shaped us into Man.
 So still we shall be, surely, at the last,
Dreamless, untouched of Blessing or of Ban!

Ah, strange it seems that this thy common thought
How all things have been, ay, and shall be nought
 Was ancient Wisdom in thine ancient East,
In those old Days when Senlac fight was fought,

Which gave our England for a captive Land
To pious Chiefs of a believing Band,
 A gift to the Believer from the Priest,
Tossed from the holy to the blood-red Hand![13]

Yea, thou wert singing when that Arrow clave
Through helm and brain of him who could not save
 His England, even of Harold Godwin's son;
The high tide murmurs by the Hero's grave![14]

And thou wert wreathing Roses—who can tell?—
Or chanting for some girl that pleased thee well,
 Or satst at wine in Nasha'pu'r, when dun
The twilight veiled the field where Harold fell!

---

[13] Omar was contemporary with the battle of Hastings.
[14] Per mandata Ducis, Rex hic, Heralde, quiescis, Ut custos maneas littoris et pelagi.

The salt Sea-waves above him rage and roam!
Along the white Walls of his guarded Home
 No Zephyr stirs the Rose, but o'er the wave
The wild Wind beats the Breakers into Foam!

And dear to him, as Roses were to thee,
Rings long the Roar of Onset of the Sea;
 The Swan's Path of his Fathers is his grave:
His sleep, methinks, is sound as thine can be.

His was the Age of Faith, when all the West
Looked to the Priest for torment or for rest;
 And thou wert living then, and didst not heed
The Saint who banned thee or the Saint who blessed!

Ages of Progress! These eight hundred years
Hath Europe shuddered with her hopes or fears,
 And now! — she listens in the wilderness
To thee, and half believeth what she hears!

Hadst thou THE SECRET? Ah, and who may tell?
'An hour we have,' thou saidst. 'Ah, waste it well!'
 An hour we have, and yet Eternity
Looms o'er us, and the thought of Heaven or Hell!

Nay, we can never be as wise as thou,
O idle singer 'neath the blossomed bough.
 Nay, and we cannot be content to die.
We cannot shirk the questions 'Where?' and 'How?'

Ah, not from learned Peace and gay Content

Shall we of England go the way he went
The Singer of the Red Wine and the Rose
Nay, otherwise than his our Day is spent!

Serene he dwelt in fragrant Nasha'pu'r,
But we must wander while the Stars endure.
 He knew THE SECRET: we have none that knows,
No Man so sure as Omar once was sure!

XXII

To Q. Horatius Flaccus

In what manner of Paradise are we to conceive that you, Horace, are dwelling, or what region of immortality can give you such pleasures as this life afforded? The country and the town, nature and men, who knew them so well as you, or who ever so wisely made the best of those two worlds? Truly here you had good things, nor do you ever, in all your poems, look for more delight in the life beyond; you never expect consolation for present sorrow, and when you once have shaken hands with a friend the parting seems to you eternal.

> *Quis desiderio sit pudor aut modus*
> *Tam cari capitis?*

So you sing, for the dear head you mourn has sunk for ever beneath the wave. Virgil might wander forth bearing the golden branch 'the Sibyl doth to singing men allow,' and might visit, as one not wholly without hope, the dim dwellings of the dead and the unborn. To him was it permitted to see and sing 'mothers and men, and the bodies outworn of mighty heroes, boys and unwedded maids, and young men borne to the funeral fire before their parents' eyes.' The endless caravan swept past him—'many as fluttering leaves that drop and fall in autumn woods when the first frost begins; many as birds that flock landward from the great sea when now the chill year drives them o'er the deep and leads them to sunnier lands.' Such things was it given to the sacred poet to behold, and the

123

happy seats and sweet pleasances of fortunate souls, where the larger light clothes all the plains and dips them in a rosier gleam, plains with their own new sun and stars before unknown. Ah, not frustra pius was Virgil, as you say, Horace, in your melancholy song. In him, we fancy, there was a happier mood than your melancholy patience. 'Not, though thou wert sweeter of song than Thracian Orpheus, with that lyre whose lay led the dancing trees, not so would the blood return to the empty shade of him whom once with dread wand the inexorable god hath folded with his shadowy flocks; but patience lighteneth what heaven forbids us to undo.'

Durum, sed levius fit patientia?

It was all your philosophy in that last sad resort to which we are pushed so often —

> 'With close-lipped Patience for our only friend,
> Sad Patience, too near neighbour of Despair.'

The Epicurean is at one with the Stoic at last, and Horace with Marcus Aurelius. 'To go away from among men, if there are gods, is not a thing to be afraid of; but if indeed they do not exist, or if they have no concern about human affairs, what is it to me to live in a universe devoid of gods or devoid of providence?'

An excellent philosophy, but easier to those for whom no Hope had dawn or seemed to set. Yet it is harder than common, Horace, for us to think of you, still glad somewhere, among rivers like Liris and plains and vine-clad hills, that

Solemque suum, sua sidera borunt.

It is hard, for you looked for no such thing.

124

Omnes una manet nox
Et calcanda semel via leti.

You could not tell Maecenas that you would meet him again; you could only promise to tread the dark path with him.

Ibimus, ibimus,
Utcunque praecedes, supremum
Carpere iter comites parati.

Enough, Horace, of these mortuary musings. You loved the lesson of the roses, and now and again would speak somewhat like a death's head over thy temperate cups of Sabine ordinaire. Your melancholy moral was but meant to heighten the joy of thy pleasant life, when wearied Italy, after all her wars and civic bloodshed, had won a peaceful haven. The harbour might be treacherous; the prince might turn to the tyrant; far away on the wide Roman marches might be heard, as it were, the endless, ceaseless monotone of beating horses' hoofs and marching feet of men. They were coming, they were nearing, like footsteps heard on wool; there was a sound of multitudes and millions of barbarians, all the North, officina gentium, mustering and marshalling her peoples. But their coming was not to be to-day, nor to-morrow; nor to-day was the budding princely sway to blossom into the blood-red flower of Nero. In the hall between the two tempests of Republic and Empire your odes sound 'like linnets in the pauses of the wind.'

What joy there is in these songs! what delight of life, what an exquisite Hellenic grace of art, what a manly nature to endure, what tenderness and constancy of friendship, what a sense of all that is fair in the glittering stream, the music of the waterfall, the hum of bees, the silvery grey of the olive woods on the hillside! How human are all your verses, Horace! what a pleasure is yours in the

125

straining poplars, swaying in the wind! what gladness you gain from the white crest of Soracte, beheld through the fluttering snowflakes while the logs are being piled higher on the hearth. You sing of women and wine—not all whole-hearted in your praise of them, perhaps, for passion frightens you, and 't is pleasure more than love that you commend to the young. Lydia and Glycera, and the others, are but passing guests of a heart at ease in itself, and happy enough when their facile reign is ended. You seem to me like a man who welcomes middle age, and is more glad than Sophocles was to 'flee from these hard masters' the passions. In the 'fallow leisure of life' you glance round contented, and find all very good save the need to leave all behind. Even that you take with an Italian good-humour, as the folk of your sunny country bear poverty and hunger.

Durum, sed levius fit patientia!

To them, to you, the loveliness of your land is, and was, a thing to live for. None of the Latin poets your fellows, or none but Virgil, seem to me to have known so well as you, Horace, how happy and fortunate a thing it was to be born in Italy. You do not say so, like your Virgil, in one splendid passage, numbering the glories of the land as a lover might count the perfections of his mistress. But the sentiment is ever in your heart and often on your lips.

> *Me nec tam patiens Lacedaemon,*
> *Nec tam Larissae percussit campus opimae,*
> *Quam domus Albuneae resonantis*
> *Et praeceps Anio, ac Tiburni lucus, et uda*
> *Mobilibus pomaria rivis.*[15]

---

[15] 'Me neither resolute Sparta nor the rich Larissaean plain so enraptures as the fane of echoing Albunea, the headlong Anio, the grove of Tibur, the orchards watered by the wandering rills.

So a poet should speak, and to every singer his own land should be dearest. Beautiful is Italy with the grave and delicate outlines of her sacred hills, her dark groves, her little cities perched like eyries on the crags, her rivers gliding under ancient walls; beautiful is Italy, her seas, and her suns: but dearer to me the long grey wave that bites the rock below the minster in the north; dearer is the barren moor and black peat-water swirling in tanny foam, and the scent of bog myrtle and the bloom of heather, and, watching over the lochs, the green round-shouldered hills.

In affection for your native land, Horace, certainly the pride in great Romans dead and gone made part, and you were, in all senses, a lover of your country, your country's heroes, your country's gods. None but a patriot could have sung that ode on Regulus, who died, as our own hero died, on an evil day for the honour of Rome, as Gordon for the honour of England.

> *Fertur pudicae conjujis osculum,*
> *Parvosque natos, ut capitis minor,*
> *Ab se removisse, et virilem*
> *Torvus humi pusuisse voltum:*
>
> *Donec labantes consilio patres*
> *Firmaret auctor nunquam alias dato,*
> *Interque maerentes amicos*
> *Egregius properaret exul.*
>
> *Atqui sciebat, quae sibi barbarus*
> *Tortor pararet: non aliter tamen*
> *Dimovit obstantes propinquos,*
> *Et populum reditus morantem,*

127

Quam si clientum longa negotia
Dijudicata lite relinqueret,
Tendens Venafranos in agros
Aut Lacedaemonium Tarentum.[16]

We talk of the Greeks as your teachers. Your teachers they were, but that poem could only have been written by a Roman! The strength, the tenderness, the noble and monumental resolution and resignation—these are the gift of the lords of human things, the masters of the world. Your country's heroes are dear to you, Horace, but you did not sing them better than your country's Gods, the pious protecting spirits of the hearth, the farm, the field, kindly ghosts, it may be, of Latin fathers dead or Gods framed in the image of these. What you actually believed we know not, you knew not. Who knows what he believes? Parcus Deorum cultor you bowed not often, it may be, in the temples of the state religion and before the statues of the great Olympians; but the pure and pious worship of rustic tradition, the faith handed down by the homely elders, with that you never broke. Clean hands and a pure heart, these, with a sacred cake and shining grains of salt, you could offer to the Lares. It was a benignant religion, uniting old times and new, men living and men long dead and gone, in a kind of service and sacrifice solemn yet familiar.

---

[16] 'They say he put aside from him the pure lips of his wife and his little children, like a man unfree, and with his brave face bowed earthward sternly he waited till with such counsel as never mortal gave he might strengthen the hearts of the Fathers, and through his mourning friends go forth, a hero, into exile. Yet well he knew what things were being prepared for him at the hands of the tormenters, who, none the less, put aside the kinsmen that barred his path and the people that would fain have held him back, passing through their midst as he might have done, if, his retainers' weary business ended and the suits adjudged, he were faring to his Venafran lands or to Dorian Tarentum.'

Te nihil attinet
Tentare multa caede bidentium
Parvos coronantem marino
Rore deos fragilique myrto.

Immunis aram si tetigit manus,
Non sumptuosa blandior hostia
Mollivit aversos Penates
Farre pio et salienta mica.[17]

Farewell, dear Horace; farewell, thou wise and kindly heathen; of mortals the most human, the friend of my friends and of so many generations of men.

---

[17] Thou, Phidyle, hast no need to besiege the gods with slaughter so great of sheep, thou who crownest thy tiny deities with myrtle rare and rosemary. If but the hand be clean that touches the altar, then richest sacrifice will not more appease the angered Penates than the duteous cake and salt that crackles in the blaze.'